Things Are Gonna Get UGLY

HILLARY HOMZIE

ALADDIN MIX
NEW YORK LONDON TORONTO SYDNEY

ALADDIN M!X
Simon & Schuster Children's Publishing Division
1230 Avenue of the Americas, New York, NY 10020
First Aladdin M!X edition June 2009

For information about special discounts for bulk purchases, please
contact Simon & Schuster Special Sales at 1-866-506-1949
or business@simonandschuster.com.
The Simon & Schuster Speakers Bureau can bring authors to
your live event. For more information or to book an event contact
the Simon & Schuster Speakers Bureau at 1-866-248-3049
or visit our website at www.simonspeakers.com.
Designed by Tom Daly
The text of this book was set in Arrus.
Manufactured in the United States of America
2 4 6 8 10 9 7 5 3
Library of Congress Control Number 2008934660
ISBN 978-1-4169-7563-2
ISBN 978-1-4169-9507-4 (eBook)

To the graduate program in children's literature at
Hollins University, and especially to Professor J.D. Stahl,
whose magical Myth and Folktale class inspired this book—
my take on the tale of King Tarush Beard

Breaking Protocol

I know how to restrain myself. Some other people aren't so lucky. Like Maggie Milner, who styles her drab brown hair so it curls under her chin. Maggie thinks it makes her look bouncy. Really, she looks like a dried porcini mushroom. Or there's Winslow Fromes, who's wedging into his desk, his shirt hiked up in the back, revealing a band of freckled flesh above *SpongeBob* underwear.

Some people just don't get it. I do. I get that right now I need help on the social studies test, which means I'll have to make public contact with Winslow. Some students are chatting in little clumps around the room, while others are hunched over textbooks, cramming. For me, it's too late for cramming.

"Just let me glance at your answers to the multiple choice," I say to Winslow. His thick fingers tap the little tuft of hair on his lower lip. But he's not saying anything like, *Sure, Taffeta!* or *Anything you want, Taffeta!* Can Winslow really be that stunned that I have spoken to him?

While Mr. Dribble, social studies tyrant, shakes his fist at the intercom, there's another announcement (something about free doughnuts tomorrow to celebrate another great standardized-test-score victory at La Cambia Middle School, home of high achievement). Winslow continues to ignore me. What *is* his problem? He's reading from his scrubby black notebook that he guards like it's the latest video player.

Leaning forward, I hold my cell under my desk and text Caylin and Petra. First, I google images of a zombie, then send the link and type WINSLOW.

I sniff Winslow's soapy smell and breathe on his neck so that the hairs that have fallen out of his ponytail blow upward like chick fluff. Surely, *that* ought to do the trick. But he continues to gaze straight into his notebook, which is covered in pictures of the undead and metal-clad warriors, and then, finally, mumbles something that sounds like, "Wow, I dunno. Maybe. Got to think. . . . I dunno."

All the eyes in the class swivel toward the door as the Girls make their BIG entrance. Something I've taught them well.

The Girls: An Insider's Guide

Caylin Barnes. Five feet two inches. Elbow-length bouncy blond hair usually pulled back into a ponytail. Upturned nose. Blue eyes. Has taken jazz dance since she was two and three-quarters, although she's a klutz, which makes her the bravest human being I know. Adept at secretly studying but prone to nasty stomach cramps. Charms frumpy teachers after class who are desperate for a little glamour.

Petra Santora. Five feet eight inches. Dark brown hair highlighted "Tawny River" every six weeks at The Arrangement with Roxanne, the hair goddess. Green eyes. Linebacker physique. Not afraid to wear wedge sandals. Wants to be a meteorologist or daytime anchor when she grows up because she wants to do something important on TV but doesn't care much for the news.

* * *

Caylin smiles at me and Petra rolls her eyes at Mr. Dribble as they glide into class with the newly xeroxed tests cradled in their arms and drop the bundles onto the front table.

"Put on your happy faces, folks. It's test time!" trills Mr. Dribble, who's blocking up the intercom with purple masking tape apparently so he'll never be able to hear another announcement again. The man acts strange—like a deranged game show host. His real name is Mr. Drabner. John T. Drabner, but to students he's privately just called Dribble. Mostly because of his habit of dribbling food out of the corners of his mouth and talking too much.

The rest of the class are in their seats now, sitting upright, eyes forward, holding freshly sharpened pencils as Mr. Dribble scans the room, oblivious to his static-cling polyester pants. "Whoops," he says, covering his mouth. "Some of you didn't hear me say there's a test, did ya? Because of the *constant* interruptions!" His eyes, which are the color of olive pits, glare accusingly at the taped-up intercom. Then he stops in front of *my* desk, gazing at me directly with his loopy mustache woobling up and down. "Well, surprise!" He throws up his arms. "There is, in fact a test today that *nothing* will get you out of." For a moment, with his coffee-stained teeth, he grins at Justin Grodin. Last year, Justin pulled the fire alarm seven times to get out of tests until somebody figured it out.

I glance at Caylin as she winces at the big capital letters on the board that say, TEST TODAY! I get a text from her:

`Wish I culd hlp u`

Under my desk, I thumbjockey back:

☹

Any moment now, I'm going to have to become an expert on the Articles of Confederation when I didn't have time to read that chapter. Last night, I had swim practice until 5:00 p.m. and then helped Caylin through another boy drama. My stomach muscles belt together so tightly I'm afraid I'll need an oxygen mask to revive.

"Winslow," I whisper frantically. "You've got to help me. Pleeeease. It's like a life-or-death thing." My mother will cancel the limo she's reserved to take my friends and me to Winterfest on my birthday if I don't pass the test. Of course, my dad would be semicool about it but that doesn't help since he's down in L.A. now—permanently stuck in traffic.

Sitting in the front row, Olivia, the medieval poet wench, scowls and shakes her calligraphy pen at me, spraying ink on her flowing velvet dress. Just because she said no the last time I asked her if she could assist me doesn't mean I can't give someone else the opportunity. If she doesn't want the reflected popularity I offer, it's her loss.

Winslow flips his eyelids so I can see the insides of his lids, which are all red and veiny. In a loud voice, he cracks, "Why do dwarves have such big nostrils? Look at the size of their fingers!" Then he snort laughs.

"Winslow, shut up. Just show me your paper."

"Wow," he says, tapping his pen on his chin. "You sound stressed."

Uh, yeah. Welcome to my life.

As Mr. Dribble hunches over, carefully counting out his precious social studies tests, which are thick and full of multiple staples, as if they needed to be brought under control by force, I kick the back of Winslow's chair. "I'll do anything. I swear."

Winslow swivels his head in my direction and gives me real eye-to-eye-lock. He seems like a creepy super villain with X-ray vision.

Smile, I tell myself. You're in control, on top of

your feelings—otherwise, EVERYTHING going on, like Mom and Dad and the move, will spew out. Like when you're drinking soda and crack up at a joke and bubbly stuff gushes out of your nostrils.

Petra and Caylin peer at me, all worried. They've seen me negotiating with Winslow so I wink at them and pretend I'm not in full panic mode.

As Mr. Dribble bounds toward the class, Winslow unflips his eyelids. "You mean that, Taf? About doing *anything*?"

I speak quickly and in a very low voice. "Yeah. Whatever."

As Winslow clears his throat, I get that sinking feeling in my stomach.

I'm about to become the girlfriend of Chewbacca, as in that long, hairy creature from *Star Wars*.

Chewbacca's Girlfriend

"Okay, tell me, then," says Winslow. "Tell me something you'd like to do."

I'm absently tapping on my cell phone key pad, thinking. "Something I'd *like* to do?" There is nothing—NOTHING—I'd like to do with Winslow Fromes except get VERY far away from him. But I have to come up with something that would please him and not absolutely disgust me. Blinking at the Winterfest poster taped to the cinder block wall, I babble, "Um, well, like, Winterfest is coming up, so I could . . ."

"Dance with me?"

"Sure," I hear myself saying. "Okay. Whatever. One dance. Not a slow one, though." That would involve bodily contact. Today, his T-shirt shows a hotel door with a sign that says ALREADY DISTURBED. I get a sudden panicky feeling like I'm about to be trapped in a dark, broken elevator in an abandoned hotel.

Winslow is staring at me, but not yet responding, so as Mr. Dribble hands out tests to the front row, I commit further blurtation: "You can even ride with us to the dance in a Hummer limo."

He gazes into my eyes and smiles so big I can see all of his molars, which have silver fillings in them. *"D'accord, ma cherie,"* he says, "Which translates into, 'Okay, my dear.'" Then he winks. "You got it."

Outside Math

As The Girls gather around me after social studies, I stare at my boots, which are so peanut butter suede I could eat them—they are that delicious to look at. But right now, I want to hurl. We're standing outside in the hallway, and I don't have my jacket so I'm freezing. When I say "outside" I mean *outside* outside. All of the covered hallways are in the open at La Cambia. Something I had to get used to when I moved to the West Coast from Philadelphia.

"How'd the test go?" asks Caylin. It's okay to be asking about schoolwork publicly because everyone is packed into the halls and it's hard to hear a thing. Of course, I don't need to ask Caylin how she did. She always gets As.

Petra elbows me in the shoulder. "I saw you all talking and scoping on Winslow's answers."

"Did you cheat?" asks Caylin, her voice rising. For a moment I think she's upset but then she's smiling at me. "Did you? 'Cause you're just so good at being sneaky, you sneakster."

"Whatever. It was no big deal," I say, staring at the palm trees lining the back of the amphitheater. I'd love to climb one and get away. What had I just promised Winslow? What was I thinking? Obviously, I wasn't!

Caylin steps forward so we're almost nose to nose. "Look at me. No, *look* at me and tell me you're okay." And I do. I look right into her perky blue eyes, which makes me insist that I'm fine. Caylin, with her freckled ski-jump nose and rosy cheeks, resembles a very cute elf. Half the time, I expect her to be making toys for Santa Claus.

A pack of sixth-grade boys moves past us in the hall and Petra pats a fuzzy-haired one on the head. I know he's grateful. Suddenly, Petra squeezes my arm. "You are going to so luuv the b-day prezie I got for you. Let's just say everyone will be saying 'Gucci Gucci goo' when they see you stepping out of the limo."

Limo? LIMO? As things are now I will also be stepping out with Winslow. The only thing anybody will go is "EWWWW!" What happened to me? As it is, this limo is a big splurge for my mom. I hate to ruin her efforts. Why didn't I offer him something simple like a double fudge brownie? I see the banner taped to the gym.

LAST CHANCE TO BUY TICKETS FOR LA CAMBIA PARENTS' CLUB HOUSE TOUR! $200 PER PERSON.

Our school is always doing some kind of fundraiser. Not that my family will be participating again anytime soon. *Okay, calm down, Taf.* But somehow, these words push out of my mouth. "Did I tell you that the Hummer is going to be the largest stretch available? Seriously, it's usually reserved for VIPs, but, girls, we got it." What I am saying? It's true, for my birthday (December 19—only seventeen more days!!!), Mom's renting a Hummer limo to go to Benihana where the servers flip knives and don't even kill you. But . . . well, I can't stop myself from further blurtation. "My dad special-ordered it. Some Hollywood people who he knows from his movie have some connections up here. Stanford grads."

The words keep bubbling out like water in an overfilled Jacuzzi.

"From his movie?" asks Petra.

"Yeah," I say. "His movie. *Free Range Cop*." He doesn't have a movie. But if my Dad actually finished writing a script it would definitely be called something like *Free Range Cop*. Luckily, I don't have to explain more because we have to go to math. The Girls are gazing at me with even more awe and I love it but I am now feeling the guilt thing.

Top Five Reasons I Have Felt the Guilt Thing Before:

1. I'm an eighth grader.
2. I told Caylin that I only wore my braces for nine months because my orthodontist, Dr. Wolf, is so

awesome. Actually, I wore my braces for two years and my orthodontist is named Dr. Silvers. But if I could have named him, he would definitely be called Dr. Wolf.

3. I am *still* an eighth grader.
4. I haven't come up with a decent idea for a new lipstick line in two days. My last idea was le Lickety Split. But I think it sounds like it splits your lips. I'm running into a dry spell.
5. I thought about kissing Justin Grodin again just to get more experience, even though he must have an overactive salivary gland or seal genes because there was so much liquid coming out of his mouth I had needed a life preserver to stay afloat.

Charm Mafia

After suffering through math and English, I finally sit down at our usual table in the cafeteria in front of the Quik Cart. For privacy, we, The Girls, perch as far away as possible from the feeding line and curious ears. This is, hands down, the best spot, and I staked it out the first day of school.

Petra eyes Maggie Milner sitting at the lower end of the cafeteria table with her two tragic wannabe friends who try their best to dress like us. She says loudly, "Could those cows at least pretend to have their own conversation and stop listening to us?"

Maggie reddens. Sitting next to us at the lunch table has been her only claim to fame.

Gazing at me through honey-colored eyes that ooze sweetness, Maggie goes, "Hey Taffeta, *love* your necklace."

"Thanks," I say.

"Your hair looks *so* good today," says one of Maggie's friends, the one who always flanks her left. I'm never sure of her name so I call her Invisible Girl. At this, I half nod. My hair looks good *every* day.

"Are those new?" asks Maggie, eyeing my boots.

"Uh-huh," I say, shrugging—as if I'd *ever* wear something old. Old is taboo at La Cambia Middle School; even the lost-in-the-seventies trailerlike buildings have been recently remodeled with sunroofs and green building materials. Petra clears her throat. This is the signal for them to turn around and let us eat our lunch and work on our decorations for Winterfest.

"This is going to make such a perfect moon," Caylin says, shaking glitter onto her paper decoration. I sip my yogurt shake and stare at our stack of

Elle Décor, *Teen Vogue*, and sheets of colored paper. I have just spent an hour scoping out the gym, thinking about decorating ideas. But, for obvious reasons, namely Winslow Fromes, I can't get into it now.

I'm sprinkling more glitter when Caylin clears her throat in a warning kind of way.

She points, and I can't believe what I'm seeing.

Insane Boy with Ponytail

"Winslow's waving at you!" Petra yells.

Yes, there in all his thickness is Winslow, in his duct-taped shoes and ALREADY DISTURBED T-shirt, waving at me.

His best friend Sneed bangs his fist on the table and stands up, swaying on his skinny legs. He looks like Abe Lincoln minus the hat and beard. "Taffeta? I've heard something very interesting about you. Winslow says that you and—"

Winslow clamps his hand over Sneed's mouth.

Noooo! Not in front of The Girls before I've had a chance to explain, not in front of Tyler Hutchins, who's absolutely cute, who wants to GO WITH ME to Winterfest and is already on TV commercials for his dad's Porche-Audi dealership. I glance over at Tyler, who is sitting with his usual swimming buddies. With his fingers he combs through his blond hair, which looks almost albino white, except for this greenish glow from too much swim-team chlorination. He asked me to go to Winterfest but I put him off because I don't like appearing too eager since EVERYONE likes him. It's all because of his being kidnapped last year.

My heart whams against my ribs, but not because I'm excited. It's sheer terror.

SHUT UP!

"TAFFETA!" Sneed booms in front of the entire cafeteria. "Winslow says he's going to Winterfest with you. In a Hummer!"

Noooo! I'm Taffeta Smith!

There is a complete silence as everyone lining up at the Quik Cart to buy something orange—a slice of pizza, bag of Nacho Cheese Doritos, mini-carrots, or maybe a *real* orange—stares at me, INCLUDING I-have-been-kidnapped Tyler Hutchins.

I can hear the crackle of Mr. Morley, the cafeteria monitor's walkie-talkie, and feel the stares of Olivia and her friend Ninai, their braces shining under the fluorescent lights. Caylin and Petra are bugging out their eyes and Tyler, who's sitting with Justin Grodin, pulls on his beautiful hair.

My lips are *le* stuck. I can't take it anymore.

Sending Out an SOS

Winslow gets a wide grin on his wide face and shrugs. "Whoops. Guess I kinda told a few people and they told some friends and their friends told some friends and voilà—oh well! *C'est la vie!*" That means "that's life" in French, only he purposely slaughters the pronunciation so it sounds like *set la veeee.*

Tyler, looking stunningly Nordic god–like in his white polo, with his white-green hair, flashing his white teeth, elbows his buddy, Justin, the bad kisser and fire-alarm–puller. Petra and Caylin stare at me as if I've broken all of the rules we've ever believed in.

This is all much worse than I feared.

I want to scream. But that would be uncouth.

Petra throws up her arms in complete disgust. "Were his parents siblings? I can't believe he thinks *you'd* actually say yes to going to the dance with him."

"Can you say *hallucination* or what?" says Caylin, twirling her finger in the air.

"So, Taf, what will you be wearing?" Winslow asks, his voice cracking with newly discovered hormones.

I can't say anything. The truth is I don't know what I'm going to wear because Mom won't buy me the $550 Max Heeder top I picked out. She says the price is obscene.

I can tell you exactly what and who is obscene. . . .

Winslow Fromes!

To put a stop to catastrophe, I march up to Winslow, who's standing next to the Quik Food cart. Petra and Caylin shuffle after me. I stare at Winslow's freaky black notebook. He's actually flipping through the pages right now. What could possibly be in that thing? A lady elf in a bikini?

"I see you looking," says Petra, like she can read my mind. "He intrigues you, doesn't he? Admit it."

"No," I hiss, even though I know she's joking. He doesn't interest me at all. He wears a chain on his belt that clanks down the hall. Yesterday, he posted . . .

A Lame Poem on MySpace

```
Taffeta,
U r so sophisticated. U make me want 2
```

learn French. Here is how much French I've learned bcuz o my admiration 4 u:

Éclair

Soufflé

Omelet

Garbage

French fries

French kissing

Just kidding. Hee hee.

Winslow

Why did I ever tell Winslow Fromes that my grandfather is French? Now he thinks this French thing is the key to unlocking me.

Winslow reties his ponytail. It's like he's getting ready at all times to attend a Phish concert.

Petra, her lips in full pout, wheels toward Winslow. "Look, eighties reject, Taffeta has a few other guys in mind for Winterfest." She narrows her eyes and nods over to The Guy table that Tyler lords over. "Does the name Tyler Hutchins ring a bell?"

Of course Tyler Hutchins rings a bell. How many Nordic gods are there at one school with pearly teeth, good manners, and junior-Olympic green hair, in car commercials, who have triumphed over kidnappers?

Winslow moves his brows up and down like he's Groucho Marx and puts his drinking straws in his hair like antennae. "Guess Tyler will be *jalouse* since I'm so sophisticated. *Non?*" Would he stop trying to speak French? Would he please stop talking to me in front of everyone? Winslow reaches out a hand. It's approaching my shoulder. If I don't move out of the way soon it'll be a direct hit. I sway to the left but it's too slow. His large paw grazes my shoulder.

Protocol breach!!

No!!

"Just get it out of your head, Winslow! This fantasy of me and you. Forget what I might have said. It's NEVER EVER happening!"

Winslow's face goes pale, and his lips fold into this pathetic upside-down *u* shape. Then he growls, leans over to me, and utters, "I'm so over you." Pressing his fingers against his nose, he lopes away.

Winslow actually looked really upset. He should have adhered to protocol.

Normal

Leadership class is a blur. Miss Bines lets us talk most of the period while she flips through bridal magazines for her upcoming wedding extravaganza and fiddles with her triple-pierced ears. Since we already did our leadership stuff during math anyway it's no biggie. I'm relieved Winslow takes computer for his elective because I would DIE if he were suddenly in Leadership, which I feel confident he'd never get into anyway because it's for people who feel strongly about school spirit and I've NEVER seen Winslow dress in orange and blue for La Cambia school spirit day, not even once.

I feel SO relieved to talk about normal stuff like my upcoming b-day complete with Hummer limo. Taking out the *San Francisco Chronicle* magazine ad, I stare at my Hummer.

Hummer Stretch
*22 passengers
*Black or white
*Full equipped with 1500-watt stereo system CD/DVD player and iPod dock
*Four flatscreen TVs
*Moonroof
*Fiber-optic mood lights and strobe lights
*Complimentary beverages

*Three hour minimum
*20% gratuity

After much excruciating thought and pondering, I've finally settled on black as the color. White just seemed too weddinglike.

Little Things

In science, I am doing something with a group of girls that involves a microscope and paramecia. At least Maggie is willing to score props and write up the lab for us. I think paramecia are scary and I fear what would happen to the world if they got human size.

Winslow keeps on throwing me these really nasty looks, which, I'm sorry to say, is completely uncalled for. Do you see me doing the same to him? No, I'm being completely mature about this and not alerting Mr.—oh, Mr. Something. I'm still not sure of my science teacher's name. There are a lot of teachers in this school!

For Real?

"Ready, girls?" I ask, as we stroll up the decomposed granite driveway, which is lined by these massive palm trees, to my house, a large French Colonial. Whizzing down the hill on skateboards, some seventh-grade guys are trying to hit hummingbirds with rocks. The idiots are helmetless, of course.

"If they're trying to impress us, it's REALLY working," I say sarcastically, as the taller of the skateboarders is almost hit by a large white Mercedes.

"I LOVE DEAD BIRDS!" yells Petra.

"IT'S SO HOT!" adds Caylin.

We all crack up as the boys skate away, heads down, rocks dropping from their fingers. I'm glad the boys are gone. Most of all, I'm thrilled to be rid of Winslow for the day. It's like I could write my own Declaration of Independence.

I look up at my house which won't be mine much longer. In fact, tomorrow, the packers come and relocate all of our belongings into the Sierra Garden Apartments. I swallow hard and my stomach burns. It's so hard to think about leaving this place. I love the steel blue wooden shudders, and the gray tiled roof that slopes over the top-floor windows like eyelids. Somehow I can't imagine having Caylin and Petra over to the Sierra Garden apartments.

This is the last time, I think. The very last time I can have my best friends over at my real house. My true home where both of my parents once lived with me, predivorce.

I close my left eye, trying to block out the dumb Coldwell Banker Realtor's sign—the one with Petra's mother, Aldea Santora, Realtor CRS, GRI, CLHMS Luxury Home Marketing Specialist, smiling, and the SOLD sign hanging down by the little chain—but it's still there.

It's a great house, close to Sharon Heights Park, high enough in the hills that in the backyard you can see the Bay and the Oakland hills beyond. Fog clouds the mountains, and the city of Menlo Park below is blanketed in so many trees you'd think it was a forest of pine and eucalyptus. You can even see the Stanford Tower and imagine all of the cute guys swarming the campus.

I grab my keys, open the front door, which looks like a bar of Hershey's milk chocolate, and let Caylin and Petra into the house. We pass through the near-empty living room and kitchen and meander into the great room, sitting down onto the only couch. Dad took the sectional and coffee table with him to Santa Monica because after we move we're not going to have room in the apartment. With packing boxes lining the rooms, and the pictures off the walls, the house feels embarrassingly undressed to me.

Soon, Caylin is sitting at the computer table,

working on some algebra problems and glancing at her list of potential volunteers for Winterfest. She's probably the best person I know at multitasking because her mother always has her signed up for at least ten activities. Petra's taking an inventory of the decorations we still need and I'm flipping through some magazines, trying to get some ideas.

Real Names

It's hard to believe Caylin and Petra were almost not my friends. Two and a half years ago things were very different. We had been living in Narbeth, which is right outside of Philadelphia, when Dad got an offer with Apple Computers, so we moved across country to California. I was so different then, read all of the time, and had one best friend, Claire. We mostly went around looking for sparkly rocks to add to our collection and trying to spy on people like in *Harriet the Spy*. My first day at La Cambia, Maggie the Mushroom showed me a map she had made of lunch.

Purples: Cool kids by the Quik Cart
Reds: Pretty cool
Black: Outcasts along the perimeter reading, or writing on their hands

I knew right then I wanted to be Purple—having everyone look at me, talk to me. I wanted to be adored the way Maggie the Mushroom adored the Purples. The next day, I came to school and changed my name from Ernestine to Taffeta. Taffeta is a kind of silk, and yes, it's expensive. But that's moi. I have expensive taste. I don't even need to know the price of something when I'm in a store because, every time, I'll pick out the priciest thing there. It's a disease. I'm going to have to get rich or marry rich when I get older. I know that. It didn't take long for me to bury Ernestine until I couldn't remember her anymore. I became Taffeta.

The Man Plan

Caylin flops down next to me on the couch and pushes against me. "Greenland fourteen," she squeals and we all start howling. It's this reference from sixth grade when fortune-telling boxes were the latest. You picked four boys you could marry, four places you could live, four numbers of kids you could have, and four types of houses, and from that your life was predicted. No doubt you'd always list the best, cutest boys like Tyler Hutchins and Justin Grodin and then, before you could stop them, someone would write down Winslow Fromes, just to mess with you. Back then, Winslow didn't have a ponytail but he was tubby, with Pokemon T-shirts that were too tight and revealed the contours of his man-boobs. He'd race up to anyone, telling dumb space knock-knock jokes, and then, cracking up, his cheeks flushed like strawberries, his eyes practically shut into slits, would collapse onto the floor.

Anyway, once I got stuck in the game with "marrying Winslow, having fourteen kids, living in a tree house in Greenland." And every time Winslow would pass by me, Petra would call out "Greenland fourteen," and we'd all go crazy laughing. It became a thing I got tired of. I wanted to scream *STOP IT!* a thousand times, but I didn't. I just don't do things like that. Everyone expects me to be immune from normal, everyday annoyances like Winslow Fromes.

"She's a geek magnet," proclaims Petra, smiling conspiratorially with me.

"I know," says Caylin, "What's up with that? Why do the nerds like you so much?" For a moment, I fear they're reading my mind or something. It's like they know I used to spend my days splitting open rocks looking for crystals and rereading *Harriet the Spy*.

Caylin gets a big gummy smile on her face. "So who are you going with to the dance? Seriously."

I can't handle this anymore so I toss out a complaint as a distraction. "Giving out *tests* during December is SO annoying," I say, thinking of Mr. Dribble's dumb social studies test. As I clear my throat to tell them just how freaky Dribble truly is, I feel a tap on my shoulder. Something about the hand feels heavy, and adult.

I whirl around to face . . .

My Big-Mouth Mom

My mother. Yes, my mother, Phyllis Finelli Smith, toting a tripod and giant black cameras slung around her neck. When she said she was taking photography classes in the afternoons and evenings, I had no idea she would pop up at the house during daylight hours. She's not even wearing real pants. She's wearing flowery flannel PAJAMA bottoms that she bought at the thrift store in East Palo Alto. If my mom looked like Petra's mom, the Realtor Aldea Santora, who has a blond bob and was on ads for Coldwell Banker that said MAKE YOUR DREAMS COME TRUE, she might be able to pass in those pants.

Her mantra is: "It's just a pair of pants. Does it matter what label they slap on it?"

Yes.

"If they fit well, does it matter if they're meant for daywear or sleepwear?"

Yes.

"Does it matter that someone else wore it?"

Yes, when it is someone else you don't know, a stranger who could have some rare and contagious disease.

I remember when we first moved to California, before the divorce, when my parents were in luuuuuuv, Mom used to buy her mauve lip liner from the Laura Mercier counter at Nordstrom at the Stanford Shopping Center, and go to spinning class in tight leggings and a matching low-cut V-neck top. Now she's graduated to stretch pants with elastic waistbands and oversize tees.

It's as if she's given up. She could be that way again.

Mom blinks hard like there's something in her contact lens. Her breath smells like sesame sticks which no doubt she has been hoarding again. "When I was standing in the entranceway, I heard you mention something about a test." At the very mention of the word, my heart goes all flip-floppy. "You had a test today, Taffeta?"

"Uh, yea-ah. I studied for it, Mom." I am staring at the Whole Foods bag of sesame sticks she has hidden by the floor. It is all eaten. Of course, she didn't ask me or my friends if we would like some sesame sticks. Not that we would, but most likely, this is the last of the snack food since she hasn't been grocery shopping in a week. She claims with the move it doesn't make sense to shop so we have been eating all of these bizarre things in the pantry like canned pears and boxed curry rice with raisins.

"You studied? Really?" asks Mom, her eyebrows raised. "Okay, I'm going to trust you on this one." Her voice rises. I hate when she gets all weird and parent-y on me.

"Mom, we're kinda in the middle of a Leadership meeting. But I'm surprised you're home at all."

She sets her photography equipment down on a cardboard box marked knickknacks, and glances at me so that her eyebrows knit together into a unibrow. "You know, I'm not happy with your attitude lately, Taffeta. We're in the middle of a move here, and you're not exactly helping. Maybe there would have been a better place to meet." Her eyes flick over to Petra and Caylin. "Like one of your friends' houses where they aren't in the middle of packing." Her green eyes go squinty and she clenches her jaw.

"As far as I knew, this was *still* our house," I snap.

She glares at me, and for a moment I wait for a real punishment, but I know she won't do anything. She feels too guilty about leaving me alone all the time. She licks her dry lips that haven't seen lipstick in ages. She pinches her nose like she's got a headache. "Yes, of course, it's still your house. It's just that . . . I'm sorry but I'm just a little stressed. With the move and everything." She nods at the wall of boxes labeled FM for family room and CL for closet. "Can you believe it, girls? We're really out of here."

No, I cannot believe it. Please stop talking about it. I am starting to regret bringing my friends over to my house for the very last time. I have told them over and over that this move to the Sierra Garden Apartments is only temporary. Until Mom finds us the perfect condo, and when Dad's movie deal comes through we'll move into a new house.

Mom suddenly smiles brightly, which makes me nervous. "I forgot to mention this, Taf. But the yearbook advisor asked me to help shoot Winterfest, which means I'll be able to take close-ups of you at the dance on your birthday. I thought since you guys are planning the dance you could give me some insight on what kind of lighting I'll need. You have *such* good ideas."

What's she talking about? My mother is actually going to be taking photos at the dance? I give a knowing look to Caylin before asking, "Are you serious about taking pictures at Winterfest? Please say you're not."

"Could I be detecting a little embarrassment on your part?" She stomps over to her photography bag and throws it over her shoulder. "Don't worry," she says, holding up her hand. "I won't think of talking to you. I'll just talk to Tosh."

"You're taking Tosh to *my* dance?"

"Oh, forget it." Mom snaps a piece of sugarless gum in her mouth. "You'll thank me when you're forty and you have those pictures." She stuffs her dark, weedy hair into a ponytail holder. I remember when it used to look great. Whatever happened to her cutting her hair in layers? Caylin has assured me a thousand times that it is just a stage in the whole *I'm a divorced woman* saga. "When they're bummed out, they keep eating. Try to be supportive," is her mantra.

I've tried. Really. Once I went out and bought her this really great French shampoo. From the looks of it, she hasn't been using it.

"Remember when I made that mermaid birthday video?" asks Mom. "Aren't you glad we have that? I think you were turning nine. It was called *Little Mermaid Ernestine*."

My insides shrink and Mom freezes. When she glances at me, her face turns as white as the tips on Petra's French manicure.

I Am Not Ernestine

She used my real name. I can't believe it. The name that shall not be spoken. The one I was born with. How many times have I told her NEVER EVER use that name in public? She knows why. Usually my real name is like Bigfoot. It does not exist. But now Bigfoot is back from my Big-Mouth Mom.

Mom furrows her unplucked eyebrows. She puts her hand on my shoulder. "What's the matter with you today? What can I do?"

"Be invisible," I hiss under my breath, thinking I will never just show up and blabber to my kid's friends at key bad moments with bushy hair and elastic waistband pajama bottoms. *But that is not what you do, is it, Mom? You are always opening your Big Mouth and I am constantly shutting it.*

For a moment, she pauses, and for a moment,

I feel myself flinch at the pain in her face. "I get it," she says, clutching her photography equipment and storming out of the family room. I can hear her muttering, "I'm definitely going to talk to Tosh about this." Some people go to therapy, my mother goes to Tosh, Reiki healer, medium, and spiritual advisor. Okay, I feel a little bad, but not bad enough to run after her. Maybe if nobody else was in the house.

Maybe in a different life.

Uh-Oh

And that's when I think about how I didn't really have anyone. To go to the dance, that is, with everyone expecting me to make the BIG appearance in the limo on my birthday.

Sure, Tyler Hutchins had asked me, and I had put him off to play it cool—but not for long. I mean, the truth is, I've never had an actual boyfriend. Just guys, like Justin Grodin with too much saliva, that I've kissed at a party.

As I sit on the couch, The Girls crowd around. They want to hear about my next move. "Tomorrow's Tyler's lucky day," I say, "since I'm going to talk to him at lunch."

Condemned

Somehow, I make it through my morning classes and through most of lunch avoiding direct contact with Winslow Fromes. I take a breath and decide, yes, after gym, I'm going to talk to Tyler about Winterfest. Not that he's going to say no. It's just that I'm sick of everyone watching me all of the time. It's like I'm on stage and I'm not supposed to blow my lines.

At least being in gym always calms me and makes me feel confident because it's just a place I totally excel. Right now, I'm standing in front of the free throw line, ready to take a shot when suddenly there's a man hovering over me.

That Man is Mr. Dribble

"I need to speak with you, Ms. Smith."

Whenever any teacher uses your last name, it's *definitely* not a good sign. We're not talking extra credit and a smiley face here. And it's most definitely even worse when that teacher shows up in the middle of your gym class—the only class I don't worry about because there are no tests.

Dribble knows. Dribble knows I cheated. But he's never figured out anything before. How many times have I texted all of the questions for Petra and he's NEVER once caught me?

In the bleachers reading a book, with another excuse to get out of gym, sits Olivia Marquez. Her long, straggly, hennaed hair shields her eyes, but I can still see that she's got this funny little smile on her face and looks absolutely, disgustingly happy, which is very strange because the girl is ALWAYS depressed. She told him. I can tell. That poet wench told him I copied off of Winslow Fromes.

Olivia bites down on her tongue, smiles, and begins to mutter something that sounds like "fodderus frot." I bet it's some kind of ancient incantation. I feel a little chill.

She deserves what we did to her last year. All of it! A couple of months ago, she started speaking only in Old English. By the water fountain right outside the music room, I once found a poem that she wrote in iambic pentameter in curly calligraphy, saying how we were as dry and as superficial as Cheetos. Petra and I finally got her back. We wrote fake love e-mails to her from Tyler. She totally bought it because, the next day, Olivia taped milk-chocolate hearts and a poem about purple falcons to his locker. Last I checked falcons are NOT a big turn-on item for guys.

As Mr. Dribble glares at me, Olivia stands up, shaking her skinny arms so that her peasant blouse billows like it might fill up and carry her away like a hot-air balloon. I wish it would. She squints her medieval eyes at me and then smiles at her dorky, community-activist friend Ninai Levine, who's actually wearing her girl scout uniform—white shirt, khaki pants, and a sash. Does she understand this is eighth grade, which is practically high school, which is almost college?

I glower at Olivia as she grins and pushes all of her bracelets up her arm, jingling. Really, if I were cadaver-pale and wore tentlike peasant clothing, I don't think I'd wear jangly jewelry to call attention to myself!

Petra and Caylin give me looks of sympathy. Gracefully, I throw a basketball up in the air as a final punctuation mark to the moment. The ball spins in the net, rattles the hoop, and bounces out of the basket. *Blahh!* Outside one of the gym windows, I stare at the fields, which are permanently green, even in the summer, because of the extensive watering system donated by the very generous La Cambia Parents Club.

Dribble smiles so big you can, unfortunately, see

his yellow teeth, and his bushy mustache wriggles like a guinea pig. "I'm waiting, Ms. Smith. Collect your things and let's go back to the classroom. *Now.*" Patting down his comb-over, he folds his arms across his chest and taps his foot.

"I've heard he's kicked out five kids from school just this year," says Petra under her breath.

"He's *such a meanster,*" Caylin whispers, then gives me a half smile. "Don't worry, we've got your back."

A Fresh Start

Mr. Dribble bites into his sandwich and holds up two papers. One has my name on it. The other, Winslow's. "Can you explain this?"

The room smells like Spam and Dr Pepper. "Look, I'm *so* sorry. It's just that my birthday's coming up and I was planning—" I can barely choke out the words. There are no words. When you cheat, the school rule is that you go on N.P. (no privileges), which means you can't attend any school functions such as dances, which means no Winterfest!

Mr. Dribble pulls a pickle out of a jar on his desk. He crunches down onto the green, pimpled spear, and juice runs down his chin.

I start to cry now. Chest heaving. Tears streaming.

Room spinning. "All of my friends will be there. I rented a limo. We're going to Benihana. We're going. Oh. I—just tell me what you're going to do."

Chugging from a Dr Pepper, Dribble paces in front of his desk, which is cluttered with Ziploc bags from his lunch and tissues. "You know what you need? A CYT file." He takes a bite out of his sandwich.

I'm so confused. A file? CYT? What was the man talking about? "A CYT file? What's that? Are they down in the office?"

Dribble laughs so hard he snorts and a bit of sandwich flies out. Ewwwwwww!

"Want to know what a CYT file is?" he asks. "It's a Cover Your Tracks file. Lots of folks don't know about it."

I try to figure out what all of this means. What is he talking about?

Aha!

Dribble inhales another bite of his sandwich. He chews on the left side of his mouth and makes a popping sound. "There's lots of folks who are real smart and educated but they'll leave their hot ashes in a double paper bag and set it on their wooden deck and wonder why their house catches on fire. It's called common sense."

He gazes out the little bit of window at the top of the cinder block wall. "The fog's about burned off by now. Good for ducks." Winking, he rips open a Hostess Twinkie and stuffs it whole into his mouth. I don't get this man. What does this all mean? Well, for one thing, since my eyes are all teary my mascara is probably running.

Dribble opens his mouth to talk, revealing Twinkie cream on his right front tooth. "See, you're upset. We don't want that. I want to help you out. My accountant told me I'm the only honest person in San Mateo County. With my consulting business, I used to report every tip and bit of money coming my way. My accountant told me to go to a restaurant with a mirror behind the counter so I could see the drawers of the register after I paid in cash. And sure enough, I watched them pocket the cash and push 'no sale.' Then I walked around feeling like a giant lollipop. A huge sucker. After that, I did what everybody else was doing. I got smart." He peers at me. "Wouldn't you say that I got smart?"

"Uh, yeh-aah." I still had no idea what he was talking about.

He chews extra slowly like he's assessing something. Suddenly, Dribble jumps in front of his desk. "How would you like a chance to do things differently?" His mustache wags and I can see his banana-colored teeth again. "A fresh start?"

What does that mean? "Like a complete do-over?"

He smiles fully so that the yellowness is now overpowering. "Yup. A *complete* do-over."

I nod, thinking about him canceling out that test, letting me retake it after winter break and pretending like none of this ever happened. "Wow. That'd be amazing."

"Whenever I think you're ready for the fresh start, it can happen. We're talking about a glimpse of a whole new world." It's just a test. What the heck is he talking about now?

"So you're going to erase what I did," I rephrase, just to make sure I'm getting this. It seems too good to be true.

"Mmm-hmm. If you're really sure that's what you want to do." He glances at me, arching his eyebrows so they practically touch his hairline. *Am I sure that's what I want to do? I'm sure I'm sure. Is the man crazy? Who wouldn't want that?*

"Yes. I'm *so* there."

"Okay, if that's what you *really* want," he says, adding an extra syllable to the word "really."

I try to take in the meaning of this, to make sure my ears aren't playing tricks. He smiles big so I will get his drift. I do. I stand there, in total awe. Hallelujah! Yes! Yes! Yes! It's a bonafide miracle. Everything's going to be okay, I think, glancing up at the pinholes in the ceiling, then down at the dry-erase board filled with dates and facts comparing and contrasting the Magna Carta with the Mayflower Compact. More than okay. Mr. Dribble isn't mean. They have it all wrong. He is truly an excellent teacher and deserves every accolade available to a middle school educator. I try to take in everything and freeze-frame the moment. The way that the fire alarm evacuation map is stapled crooked on the bulletin board, even Mr. Dribble's Spam sandwich and sour dill pickles.

My life is converging upon perfect.

"Thank you. Thank you *so* much. I *promise* you won't regret it."

"I *know I* won't." I can imagine him soon tearing up my paper. The ripped-up shreds that used to be my test will flutter like snowflakes into the pine green trash can.

"A fresh start," he says in a trancelike tone.

"Everything will be wiped clean. You'll be like a whole new person."

A deep cold shoots through my veins. My body feels all tingly, as if I have the chills. My legs shake as if a tremor is rollicking under the floor, and little pinpricks of static energy roll through my arms and curl my toes.

'Sup?

It's so bad I have to stop next to the water fountain where the John F. Kennedy mural says something about doing stuff for your country. As fast as the chills came, they are gone.

But for some reason, my body's still jumpy from that tremor and I'm feeling jittery. How random. What *did* just happen, exactly? *Hello, you live in the Bay Area of California, Taffeta. Earthquakes, mudslides, and traffic are a part of life. Get over it.* I look around. Nobody is exactly acting all weirded-out or anything.

The bell rings, and soon everybody streams into the hallways. The bulletin boards have been newly decorated with Christmas, Hanukkah, and Kwanzaa decorations that Leadership organized. The seventh graders did a decent job putting them up, although some of the dreidels are crooked. But I'm not exactly feeling the holiday spirit, after those chills and everything.

Down the corridor, I spot Tyler Hutchins strutting over to his locker. I try to stand up straighter and stop the slight tremors in my legs. Even from a distance, he looks hotter than any other guy in the eighth grade—his white hair with its beautiful green sheen, low-rider jeans and a Boardgarten T-shirt.

I'll speak to him, my Nordic god, very soon. Tyler will be thrilled when I say yes to Winterfest.

I stroll down the hall to Tyler's locker and knock into a seventh grader. I swing back my hair and my hips. True, I don't really have hips, but life's all about illusion.

Right?

Sure enough, all of The Guys whirl around to check me out. Justin and Tyler huddle in the hallway, kicking around a hacky sack.

"Look, it's coming!" says Justin, cupping his mouth in his usual megaphone style. *It*. What is he talking about? Tyler spins around, and so do the rest of The Guys, so I smile at them with my top lip pulled taut against my whitened teeth for maximum smile effect.

"Hey!" I call out, strutting over to Tyler, and he stares at me as I put my hand on his shoulder. He takes a big gulp of air. Could the boy be intimidated by me? Probably.

I stare seductively at him, my eyes following his fingers as he scratches the long skinny scar that crawls like a caterpillar along his chin. I can't help thinking about how Tyler escaped from kidnappers. I wonder how you go about attracting robbers and letting them know you're up for ransom?

"Hey, Ty. It's me, ready to talk. This is your lucky day, bay-bee!"

Taking a step backward, Tyler crams his binder into his locker. "Afraid of that." This comment takes me totally by surprise. Usually Tyler demonstrates, like, not one iota of sarcasm or humor. He wheels around, slams his locker shut, glances down at his Nike trainers, and mumbles. "I didn't copy off you in math last week."

What is he talking about? Under my glare, he squirms. "Okay, just a little, but Justin did it first." Justin twists his face and makes a cross with his fingers like I'm a vampire. "I didn't copy off of *it*."

"Copy? It? What are you talking about? I'm terrible at math." Every morning, I get my math homework from Maggie the Mushroom's invisible friend or some number-smart person. "Math. Not my thing," I say with a wave of my hand.

The corners of Tyler's eyes crinkle. "Yeah, okay, sure, Einstein. What-evah."

"We need to talk." I raise my eyebrows as sexily as possible and swivel my shoulders so my chest is at its premium. "Alone."

Edging away from me, Tyler clenches his jaw and shoves his hands into his jeans pockets. Weird. Tyler is proving quirkier by the second. Maybe I misjudged him. Okay, I take in a little bit of breath. Normally, I never get nervous doing these things. Usually, I feel charitable giving someone a piece of my time because I'm always being pulled in ten million directions at once. "The answer is yes!"

"Yes? Yes, what?"

"Yes, I'll meet up with you at Winterfest." I give him my biggest-wattage smile. "On my birthday, you know. We're doing the limo thing. A Hummer."

"I didn't ask you."

Oh, now he's playing drama queen. Just because I made him wait. "Tyler, you're being, like, ridiculous. You dropped hints, begged me practically. The e-mail, text messages, et cetera. . . ."

"I didn't send you a thing."

"Oh, shut up!" *You did too. Liar!*

I had it memorized.

I really wish the birds outside weren't chirping. Makes everything seem happy and right now I am anything but happy. A crowd gathers around us. Now Caylin and Petra strut down the hall and circle around me. But they're whispering furiously to each other and laughing. It's like they're all in on something funny, and I'm the punch line. Sweat beads down the back of my neck. My skin prickles, my nose feels strangely heavy—because I'm wearing glasses. "What??!!!" I pull them off, and suddenly my world goes out of focus. "I've got glasses!"

"Aren't you quick," quips Petra, who in her green dress looks like a fuzzy blob of mold.

Normally, I wear my glasses only in the morning before I put in my contacts. Okay, this is weird. I really thought I put my contacts in before school. I scratch my neck like mad, which makes everyone laugh.

At me. At me? At me!

I slide the frames back on and everything becomes clear. Doors have edges and people have strange staring faces. But that isn't the really scary part. The scary part is that I'm wearing a black skirt with an elastic waist band. Elastic! And ankle socks with unicorns. I've got on some kind of polyester blouse, too, with horses jumping over fences. How had I not noticed this before?

"Someone did something to me!" I yell.

"You're tripping, Ernestine," says Petra.

Ernestine. She called me Ernestine. Why is she calling me by my old name? What is up?!!!! Staring at the cement, I speed down the hall to my special place. The place that I go when I'm sad or depressed. The place that always puts me in a good mood.

The Bathroom

Specifically, the mirror.

I dart into the bathroom. I have to see myself SOON. Taking a deep breath, I get the usual whiff of soggy paper towels, bleach, and urine. Slowly, I raise my chin to the mirror. No need to move too quickly. Soon I would see that perfectly symmetrical face, lovely green eyes with lashes so dark and long they look false, that aquiline nose without a bump, smooth skin with no blemishes, no circles under the eyes, and my long auburn hair which is always silky—so long as it's properly conditioned.

Ninai, Olivia's Girl Scout friend, bumps into me

before I can check myself out. "Remember, the Book Worms are meeting after school today," she says, actually whipping out a toothbrush and charger from her backpack.

Huh? The Book Worms, that's the name of those library helpers. Like I would do that. Ninai is always jumping into convos and making comments. I admire geeks who keep to themselves. At least they know their place. Not Ninai. She'd speak to anyone, even with an electric toothbrush in her mouth.

So now I look up, staring at the face staring back at me. There must be some mistake. I must still be washing my hands. There must be someone else looking at herself in the mirror. I open my mouth. The person in the mirror opens her mouth. I touch my nose, and so does the skeevy in the mirror.

Ninai, with her mouth full of toothpaste and looking official in her Girl Scout outfit, rushes over to me, staring intently. "What's the matter? You don't look well." She spits in the sink. "Are you sick, Ernestine?"

"Ernestine?!!!! Why are you calling me that?" My neck is perspiring again. Everything itches and my temples throb. And I think I smell a little.

Am I sick? Sick? My hair is frizzing out like I

stuck my finger in an electrical outlet, pimples dot my pasty forehead like a gravel road full of potholes and piles of dirt. I lean over so I can see my legs. I still have on those unicorn ankle socks! They are rolling down to my thickish calves, my black skirt hikes up a nondescript waist—backward! My glasses slip down my nose. When I breathe, my glasses fog up.

"No, I'm not sick!"

I am realizing something unimaginable has happened.

I Am a Geek

Clenching every muscle in my body, I hold my breath. *Make this go away.* I glance back at the mirror. I'm still a geek. Not working. I jump up and down, shake my head from side to side, splash cold water on my face, and then dump it down my neck.

Okay, now I'm just a wet geek.

I've got to get out of this school. There's only one way that I know.

The School Nurse

Mrs. Johnson briefly glances at me. She's filling up a glass full of miniature candy canes and bopping to an elevator-music version of "Jingle Bell Rock" on her radio. "What's the matter, hon?"

"Everything." I pat my cheeks, chin fat, pimples, and my head. "My hair's having a party, and I've got spillage!" I show her where a rim of fat hangs over my belt. "See!"

Mrs. Johnson cocks her head and peers at me like I'd look better if I were only sideways. "Hon, body issues are common at your age." She leafs through a bunch of brochures on a shelf, and hands one to me. "You might want to take a look at this."

The brochure features two girl linking arms, standing on the beach in tank dresses. The cover reads, *Body Issues: What you need to know about maintaining a healthy diet and lifestyle*. This poor woman thinks I am in need of counseling. "You don't understand. It's not like that. It just happened. Right after fourth period. People are calling me Ernestine."

"They would. That's your name."

I throw up my hands so I don't use them to strangle this woman. "Yes, it's my name, but it's *not* the name I use, okay? Nobody at this school has ever, *ever* called me Ernestine. Not until today, that is."

Sitting down, Mrs. Johnson stuffs herself into her chair and pulls my file up on her computer.

"Honey, I've got your name as Ernestine."

"Okay, fine. It's my, whatever, official name, but I changed it to Taffeta on my registration form in sixth grade when I came to La Cambia. That's the name you *should* have."

Mrs. Johnson hums to "Jingle Bell Rock" and pulls out a thermometer.

"Okaaaaay, I get it. This is some kind of joke or something. Ha. Ha. Very funny. You're *all* in on it."

Mrs. Johnson jams the digital thermometer into my ear. "In on what? I'm not in on anything. Hon, it sounds as if you're having some self-doubts about body image and identity. It happens eventually with most girls, sooner in your case. Maybe you want to make some changes. I'm sure you'll have a lot to talk about when your mom picks you up." Then she smiles at me. "It'll all be okay, Ernestine."

"My name is Taffeta. Taffeta Smith. I'm pretty and popular. I'm loved. Ernestine doesn't exist. Ernestine is nothing. I am NOT nothing! I am Taffeta!"

She smiles at me so that her hooded eyelids creep up. "You know, I did that when I was your age. I pretended I was Jane Fonda. Taffeta. That's a nice name. When you become eighteen, you can call yourself whatever you want."

Mom, the Rescue Hero

Okay, my mother is once again outdoing herself, and setting world records for how to embarrass her daughter. Right now she's sporting mismatched socks, a floppy crushed velvet hat with a giant poppy on the top, and a lapel pin that says, MAKE LOVE, NOT WAR.

Just a moment ago, I had been SO happy to see her. Really, I could have just kissed her a million times, because I was SO tired of this game. And waiting here with Mrs. Johnson, Christmas Muzak maniac, didn't make it any better. It made me feel CRAZY. And I'm many things. I mean, I know I have at least one fault—I'm too organized—but I'm not *crazy!*

Anyway, I threw my arms around Mom's shoulders, feeling the slippery, wrinkly polyester material. Then I tried to explain to her EVERYTHING that had happened. Of course, everything came out mumbled and garbled. But she thought—get this—that I was talking about some fantasy story I had made up.

How random. Now I stare at my mother, who thinks my life is a myth. "Can we go home?" Maybe if I take a shower it'll all go away.

Mom fingers my damp, limp hair. "It'll be okay, Little Love." When she says that, in the same way she always does, my heart stops the galloping, and my whole body relaxes. "It's okay, Ernestine," she coos.

"Ernestine?" I look up. My whole head feels unbalanced, like I just stepped off a tilt-a-whirl. "DID *YOU* JUST CALL ME ERNESTINE?"

Call Dad

"*He'll* understand what's going on," I state as Mom and I trek through the hallway. "He, of *all* people, won't call me Ernestine." We're standing in front of the trophy case and I'm gaping at my reflection in the volleyball plaque.

Mom bites her bottom lip. "Okay, look, I'm sure you can talk to *your father* when he calls on Sunday."

"SUNDAY? I *can't* wait that long. This is an emergency! I've got to speak to him *now*!"

"Be my guest. You know, you can call your dad anytime." As she's talking, I'm dialing his number on my cell. I still have that, at least.

The phone rings, and then Dad's voice mail comes on. "Hey, it's Dirk. I'm probably out doing a jog with my dog. Surf's up. Leave a message."

"Dad, it's me. Something terrible has happened.

It's *really* bad. Worse than you can imagine. Call me back right away!"

Mom reaches out her arms to me like I'm a little kid. "Can I give you a hug, Ernestine? I know how frustrating it's been for you not always being able to reach him."

"NO, this has NOTHING, do you hear me, NOTHING TO DO WITH DAD! Please go away."

Mom sucks in her breath, and then she finally opens the door leading to the pickup circle in front of the school.

I feel lost.

Knock Knock?

"There is no way I'm going to be caught dead on that," I say, folding my arms in front of my chest. In the parking lot, the one people use for cars, Mom points to her vintage bicycle built for two with lots of peeling paint and plenty of rust. "Why did you have to pick me up on that *thing*?" Ever since the divorce, Mom's gotten real serious about being green. And I'm all for the environment but not when it creates unnecessary embarrassment. I'll take the extra pollution, thank you. There's an unwritten law at La Cambia that parents (or nannies) aren't allowed to pick up kids unless they're in a new Beamer or a Mercedes. I'm serious. I've never seen anything else unless you count the four-wheel drive Volvos. But even those are a little subpar.

Mom lines up the numbers on her combination lock. "Oh, well." She throws up her hands. "Guess you'll have to stay in school, then. It sounded to me like things were *pretty* bad." She stares at her wrist as if she has a watch (which she doesn't). "I even cancelled my appointment with Tosh this afternoon to clear the deck."

"Aw, big sacrifice," I say. "Canceling with your medium. Couldn't he just like fly to you in your dreams or something?"

Mom laughs and snaps on her helmet, then hands me mine. It's pink and sparkly. "You know, the truth is I was really looking forward to today's session, but I *did* reschedule."

Reluctantly, I edge into the seat behind her and put on the helmet. Do I have a choice? I have to get away from school. Soon we are far away. We bike down El Camino Real past Kepler's Books, and, naturally, it's pouring down rain. Even though cold water lashes against my cheeks, I don't worry about my mascara running because I'm not wearing mascara—or any makeup, for that matter!

As the rain lets up, we pull up to an apartment complex, the Sierra Garden. Not that there's a garden in sight. It's the sort of run-down place where you'd expect some artistic type who didn't have a steady income to live. "Why are we going here?" I say. "Let's go home."

Mom stares at me as if I was abducted, taken into Area 51 and reprogrammed. "This is our home. Did you forget it was moving day? Paying for them to unpack and pack us was worth every penny. Even if it means the two of us tightening the belt a little for the next few months. The moving company did a wonderful job. Even the clothes are back in the drawers."

"I guess I forgot," I mumble. "About the move."

Mom squints at me. "Are you okay?"

No, I'm not okay. I'm less than myself. A ghost of me. "Since we didn't do any packing I guess I sort of made it—the move—not happen in my mind or something."

"I could see that," said Mom. "I know it's not easy."

Understatement, Mom. Über understatement. Oh no, it has happened. We've really moved to the Sierra Garden apartments. Whenever Mom would be SO mad at Dad after he'd come home super late from a meeting and then tell her that he had to go out again and train for his triathlon, she'd be the one to get on to the phone with her sister Megan and fume, "If things get really bad, I can always move with Taffeta to the Sierra Garden apartments."

At the time I thought it was a sort of fun, downsizing-your-life daydream. Why would she really want to give up our amazing home in Menlo Park for some apartment complex? I stare at the mission-style building with its red tiled roof and naked, statue-boy fountain that doesn't work in the center of the courtyard. Little kids run around in the front parking lot, totally unsupervised, from what I can tell, which is probably typical of poor people who live in apartments like Sierra Garden. If I had been a baby here I could see me now, barefoot, in a soggy diaper, heading into traffic. Why can't we have our old house back? Why? I guess the fact that we've moved into an apartment is NOTHING compared to the fact that, somehow, I'm like a TOTALLY different version of myself.

A New Day, Unfortunately

I jump out of bed and glimpse my face in the mirror

above a scratched-up chest of drawers plastered with *Lord of the Rings* stickers. Only everything's out of focus and fuzzy. I think I spot a pair of purple plastic glasses next to a stack of fantasy books on the nightstand.

I squint and instinctively push the glasses onto my face. No chintz bedspread bought with last year's birthday money at Pottery Barn. Nasty-looking clothes, such as socks with images of little dragons, litter the floor. Posters cover the walls—posters with creatures from *Star Wars* and UNICORNS!

On the walls, I see posters of MORE unicorns and a green dragon winging over a lavender volcano. I gaze at the face of the dragon and once again look at my face in the mirror that's over my bureau.

The dragon and I have a lot in common. We are both depressingly similar-looking.

I see a girl with frizzy hair, like a halo of fire. Round cheeks dotted with whiteheads. I am not looking at my mother's middle school yearbook photo.

Or Olivia.

Me. It's for real.

I jam a brush through my hair, but no matter how many times I try, my do won't cooperate. It's possessed! In desperation, I plaster my hair with gel.

I now look like I have either very wet or very greasy hair.

It's useless.

On a hook behind my door, I spy a floppy flowered hat, plop it on my head, and call it good.

Then I head over to attack the closet. It's a jumbled-up mess with clogs and old rainboots tossed haphazardly on the dusty floor. Dresses hang next to wrinkled pairs of purple pants hanging precariously on wire hangers. None of the shirts are buttoned. A box of headless Barbies and Bratz dolls sit on a shelf with pink plastic ponies, a microscope kit, and a dirty white down comforter. There's definitely nothing decent to wear in there. Wait! I spot a pair of black capris.

I yank them off the rusty hanger and put them on. I glance in the mirror, and think that I actually look semipassable. Maybe I can dress myself back into being me. The idea lifts a little hope in my chest. Turning around, I suddenly see the damage on the pants—a giant stain on the back.

I yank the pants off and throw them onto the bed. There has to be a decent pair of pants somewhere. I need makeup—no, *require* makeup. But where to find some? In the bottom of the bathroom drawer, I find a blue vinyl bag containing one lipstick, ten nail files, and a bottle of very old mascara. I dip my finger into the lipstick, spread it on my lips and cheeks, and attempt to get some color onto my pale, stubby lashes, but it looks clumpy and pathetic.

I remember this meditation I made up to help me relax when I was really little: "Am I me? Are you you? Am I me?" Wrapping my pillow around my face, I'd chant it over and over before I'd go to sleep at night. The "you" in the chant meant everybody, every living creature. At the time, when I was three or something, it made sense. I think I was a lot smarter back then. I remember later on it helped me transition into going to sleep at night even when my parents, before the divorce, were fighting, even when they were very loud, and hysterical. I'd think, *Are you you? Am I me?* until you and me blurred into one, until I felt the comfort of not being distinct.

This time not being me doesn't bring happy thoughts. This is not working.

Yesterday afternoon, after pacing around in this apartment and hoping it was all a very bad dream, I had even biked over to the pool to show up for swim practice but Coach Gina acted like she had no idea who I was. Me! Junior Olympic Swimmer. The girl who placed at Far Westerns. I am *so* not me.

I crawl into bed and bury myself deep within the comforter, waiting to disappear. For a moment, I reach out to snuggle with Napoleon, our golden retriever. But then I remember we had to put her to sleep last month. Napoleon gone. Dad down in L.A. Myself altered beyond recognition! Oh, I can feel the sadness of all humanity. The depths of despair in SpongeBob. Yet, I'm still me. At least these are my thoughts. Am I in a coma in some sort of vegetative state? A high fever?

Who's There?

It's Mom, banging on my door, calling out, "You're going to be late." Mom is telling me that I'm going to be late? Now there's a first. "Honey, get up *now*."

I don't speak. What's there to say? Her curly brown hair sticks straight up but she's fully dressed, if you can call baggy sweatpants and the same shirt she wore to bed being dressed.

I plunk down in a beanbag chair actually shaped like a spaceship.

"What's going on?" Mom asks, entering my room. This is special. Usually, she's been up too late reading books on photography and the lost worlds of Atlantis and Lemuria to be up at seven a.m. She must have been told to share some morning sunlight time with me from her medium Tosh. I think if he told her to sell shares of me on eBay, she would do it.

"I don't feel well," I say, sinking farther down into the beanbag chair. I'm not about to get into the whole I'm-not-myself thing again. Then I remember the quake. "Maybe I'm still jittery, you know, from the tremor yesterday, waiting for an aftershock, or whatever."

Mom opens my door and peers into the room. I can see the hall is filled with unopened moving boxes. "You sure?"

"Yes," I say, standing up. "It felt pretty major."

"Let me go check online because I didn't feel a thing yesterday, and I was shooting some photos for *The Palo Alto Tribune* up on the ninth floor of the VA Hospital. Believe me, if there'd been a quake that thing would've been swaying like a pendulum." Mom pads into the hallway, hopping over the boxes, down to the computer in the kitchen, and a moment later, she calls out. "Nope. Honey, nothing. Maybe it was construction or something."

Construction? I don't think so. As she closes my

bedroom door, it comes to me. It *was* something all right. I *know* I felt the floor shaking right after Dribble said he was going to help me. *Hello.* Right afterward, as in microseconds later. Earthquake. Fresh start. Dribble. Helping me. Major life change.

I think I'm getting this. Why did it take me so long to see what happened?

The direct connection jolts me, and it's like my whole body's buzzing. Quaking. Alive. But not in a good way.

Yesterday afternoon, when Dribble asked me if I wanted a fresh start, I thought he was talking about the test. Now I know better—he meant my life.

I Have to Get to School

For the first time, I'm dying to see Dribble.

But not to see me and my scary clothing. Apparently, it's not a budget reality to go to the Stanford Shopping Center and get a whole new wardrobe. Even when I very reasonably suggested a couple of small items from Max Heeder online, like their baby doll T-shirts, which are on sale for three hundred dollars, my mother declined.

With no decent choices, I pull on a pair of baggy jeans and a T-shirt that says QUESTION REALITY.

Lovely. My new motto. On a hook behind my door, I spy a purple hoodie with flowers, and put it on over my shirt. Looks-wise, I feel like I've stepped into a vat of bugs.

Is There Anybody Out There?

I slink down the hall with my hoodie pulled down over my head. Except for a custodian pushing a mop bucket down the hall, the place is deserted.

I race until I'm in front of my first-period class, social studies with Mr. Dribble, classroom number thirteen.

Of course.

How hadn't I noticed the BAD LUCK number on the door? Duh. I always knew he was a veeeery strange teacher—but completely altering someone? That's just WRONG!

I look both ways, expecting a black cat to cross my path or a ladder to crash on my head.

"Dribble! Yo, Dribble!" I bang on the door. "Hello in there!" Caylin opens the door, and I have never been so happy to see her freckled ski-jump nose and Tahoe blue eyes. "Girlfriend, I'll explain everything la-ter." She glances at me, her eyebrows raised into a question. Dribble dramatically throws up his hands.

"Welcome to class, Ernestine. I'll need your late pass, ma'am." He turns to face the rest of the class. "Anyhoo, what page did I say?" How can he act like everything is normal?

"Did you just call me Ernestine?" I ask.

"Did you just call me Dribble?" He wriggles his bushy mustache. His real name is Mr. Drabner, of course. But it's easy to forget.

Twenty-nine eighth graders sit at their desks with government books open to men in white powdered wigs. Caylin giggles, Petra makes the hand sign for "wacko," and Olivia Marquez frantically motions for me to sit down. She's wearing a red babushka scarf over her hair, and a white peasant blouse with a black smocklike apron decorated with pink rosebuds. She looks like a Russian nesting doll.

"I understand everything. About the CYT file," I state, pulling my hood farther around my face.

"CYT?" asks Dribble. "Is that like the CIA?"

The class laughs. Not that I blame them.

"You told me the day before. It means cover your—"

Olivia jumps out her seat and clamps her long, pale fingers over my mouth. "Too much cold medication," she says, apologetically. Did I hear the hint of a Russian accent? "Ernestine's not herself," she says.

That's true. Olivia's hand feels cool and smells like lanolin. I try to push it away but she's stuck to me like an octopus.

Mr. Dribble hobbles back to the board, holding his precious dry eraser. He's actually whistling "Yesterday," an old Beatles tune, as he erases an old homework assignment in one wide, sweeping flourish. How can he be so happy? *I'm completely altered, Mr. Dribble! What about you? You appear to be the same strange teacher as always, in what you call "your Donny Osmond purple socks." Why are you playing dumb???*

Finally, I pull Olivia's hand off my mouth, and before she sits down, I hear her mutter, "Nyet."

"I'm not going to just take this," I say, still standing up. Then it hits me. Olivia's incantations in gym, and now muttering things in phony Russian. Her obvious hatred of me. I wheel around and glare at her babushka-covered head. "Was it *you*? You! Those magic spells. I know it was!"

Everyone in the class goes silent. I can hear the crackle of the loud speaker. Sneed nudges Winslow, who's reading whatever is inside his notebook, while Caylin and Petra roll their eyes.

Olivia steps backward, her eyes narrow. "Me? What are you talking about? Me what?"

I leap forward, my arm swinging near her face. "You're the one! Change me back! NOW! You used your magic on me! Help me! Please! You've got to use your woo-woo powers!!"

"Woo-woo?" asks Olivia, looking around the room as if woo-woo might be a new classmate.

The class is rolling in the aisles. Everyone is just completely cracking up. Even Winslow pops his head out from his notebook and gazes at me like I've got antennae sticking out of my head.

Mr. Dribble bounds toward me, his face stop-sign red, his bushy mustache twitching like a squirrel's tail. "Ernestine, we're going to have a little talk. NOW. In the hallway." As he ushers me down the aisle and out the door, in his hands, I see he has his pink-slip pad, the one he keeps on the right corner of his desk like he's a doctor of detentions, and practically everyone goes, *"Oooh,"* at the same time. I can hear murmurs of "She's going crazy" and "She's going to get a detention." And I can hear Caylin saying "Now, that was REAL random. What's up with that?"

"This is not free time, folks," says Mr. Dribble,

through clenched teeth. "While I chat with Ms. Smith, you guys are going to be reading about Thomas Jefferson. Heard of him? The dude on the front of a nickel, third president, ringing a bell? Read pages 105 to 114. And answer the questions at the end of the chapter."

The class groans and I hear a few sarcastic, "Thanks, Ernestines." Dribble shakes his head. "Remember, you kiddos live in high-tech heaven, you got nothing to complain about. When I was kid, the number-one spot the Soviets wanted to nuke was here, the Silicon Valley. Not Washington, D.C. or New York or even Mount Rushmore, the place with the four presidents' heads. You kids now have it easy-peasy pie."

The man makes absolutely NO sense.

As we walk into the hallway, Mr. Dribble clutches his pickle jar in one hand and his pink detention-slip pad in the other. I squeeze my knuckles, trying not to let out a stress-busting primal wail.

Dribble Speaks

Mr. Dribble leans against the wall in the hallway and fishes a pickle out of his jar. "You're right as rain, Taffeta Smith."

"Right about what?"

He crunches into the pickle and juice drips down his chin. "I did it. Not Olivia. I hated hearing you give credit to the wrong person."

For a moment, I feel like I'm in freeze-frame mode but then I feel the whoosh of air flooding back into my lungs, the buzz of the fluorescent lights, the chatter in the classroom. *He did this? Mr. Dribble, who talks like a game show host, who enjoys the color purple, who loves his mustache just a little bit too much?*

My original hunch was right. I'm a quasi genius.

No, this is crazy. I have become crazy. Yet, deep down I know all of this is somehow REAL.

"Are you kidding me?" I ask, hoping that he will say yes. That it's all an elaborate hoax. That I've been punked.

"I'm an educator, Miss Smith. And right now I'm trying to educate you about the truth. I did it."

Can I really be having this conversation? Yes, apparently, I can. Mr. Dribble is smiling at me and pulling on the ends of his mustache.

Right now I want to pull the mustache off his face. "Change me back. Make me into *me*."

He winces like he's got food stuck in a molar. "Sure wish I could. Boy, do I."

"What do you mean you *wish* you could? Do your thing!"

"It's not in my control, Miss Taffeta. After all, you're the one who said you wanted a fresh start."

"I didn't mean change me into Freakzilla. I meant change what I did."

"Did?" Mr. Dribble asks.

"You know," I say under my breath. "My cheating. Not as me. As someone else. Oh, you know what I mean."

Mr. Dribble licks his yellow teeth and his orange mustache woobles. "Like I said, it's all up to you."

"Me? Something *I* need to do?" He's crunching on the pickle extra loudly and I want to tell him to close his mouth but I'm afraid he'll turn me into a rodent or something.

"Have you mistreated anybody lately?" he asks, screwing the lid on to the pickle jar extra tightly.

I think for a second. *What's he talking about? He is giving me a clue. Lucky me.*

And I think some more. *Me, mistreat someone?*

Slowly, though, a thought rolls in. "Winslow, I guess, but—"

"But nothing." He sets the pickle jar down on

the floor. "I just asked you a simple question."

Did he mean did I do something bad and now I need to do something nice to make it up? Was that it? "So I need to do something about it?" As I shake my head, frizzy strands of hair fly into my eyes. That's when it hits me—I'm really trapped in something. That my hair, as much as I brush it, isn't going to smooth down into controllable waves. It springs, it frizzes, it geeks hard. I can't do a makeover on myself to recreate Taffeta. I'm not going to be able to simply plunk contacts into my eyes and buy a whole new wardrobe. Somehow, I got into this mess magically and I've got to get out of this mess magically.

"You need to rectify," says Dribble.

"Rectify?"

"Mmm. Dancing with Winslow at Winterfest would be sweet, don't ya think?" He grins at me, and I see this huge gap in the middle of his front teeth.

"That's it? We don't have to officially go there together? Just show up independently and then I ask him to dance. He says yes, we dance, and then I'm me again?"

He scratches his chin. "Sounds reasonable."

"I thought you were going to say I had to learn

something or do something important. This is going to be SO easy." I don't even have to *go* with him to the dance, I think. Just one dance. How hard is that?

Dribble fans his pink detention-slip pad. "Easy-peasy pie. Yay, team."

"And how did you do this?" I blurt. "Who are you?"

"Who are *you*?" he asks.

I stare at him. *Infuriated* comes to mind.

Lunch

After stressing through math and English, I get in line, tray up my veggie surprise, and trudge out into the middle of the cafeteria. Kids crowd into long tables strewn with sporks, backpacks, and lunch bags. The constant chatter sounds like a dull roar. I'm not picking up a word anyone is saying. My eyes check out the lunch tables. I think of the time that Maggie the Mushroom showed me her color-coded map of the cafeteria.

Suddenly, the lunchroom becomes a rainbow of color.

Without thinking, I head to The Girls' table by the food cart. The Purples with their laughing, long hair, baby tees, whatever's cool. But then I remember.

I am still Ernestine.

My legs press against the back of Caylin's chair, and I know I must get away from here.

"Looking for your friends?" asks Petra. She points to a table near the bathroom. "Over there, Ernie."

The red wonks: poet wench Olivia and Girl Scout activist Ninai. They see me and wave me toward them.

I start to head over to Girl Geek Central, but a part of my brain screams, *Run! Get away. Once you've attached yourself to them in any way, you'll be associated forever.*

Out of the corner of my eye I see Olivia, with a dramatic intake of breath, uncap her calligraphy pen.

Instead, I head over to an empty table and sit down. I can see Ninai give Olivia a quizzical look. Sorry, but I don't have time for this, for them. There is nothing that can get me to sit with those losers.

A Sour Note

Apparently, during fifth-period elective, I'm in orchestra.

Ninai's now opening the double doors and, before I know it, I am swept into the music room along with all of the other orchestra dorks.

"You don't need to be nervous about your solo coming up," Ninai babbles. "You'll do fine in the concert." Students pluck violins, violas, and cellos as they tune their instruments.

Concert? What concert? That means I have to play an instrument I know nothing about in front of actual, live human beings. A couple of violinists play something very complicated as their fingers dance up and down the strings. I have to do that? I don't know the difference between Mozart and Beethoven. It all sounds the same to me, like the soundtrack of a movie about someone dying or a *National Geographic* special about penguins. There's just no way!

"Ernestine, are you okay?" asks Ninai.

"Um, not great. Feeling sort of sick, actually. Tell Mr.—" I point to a dude in a Beatles-like haircut.

"Mr. Takashama," finishes Ninai.

"Yeah, that guy. Tell him I'm at the nurse's office."

With that I hold my stomach and bolt out of the double doors and into the hallway, where the only sounds are the fluorescent lights buzzing.

I spend fifth period in the girls' bathroom.

Look at Me!

At the beginning of the fifteen-minute break before sixth period, I sprint to the library, figuring that's where a geek of Winslow's magnitude would be hanging out. Olivia sits at the front desk, stamping magazines that look very important and celebrity-free. I can't believe she actually takes library skills for her elective AND does that Book Worm club after school. I edge away from her and duck by a rack of paperbacks, but she's spotted me anyway.

"Ernestine, is that you?" I'm crouching and somehow my head hits the books, knocking down a copy of *Holes*.

Olivia leans over the counter. "We missed you at lunch. Are you okay?"

"Fine," I say, standing up and sliding the book back onto the rack.

"What were you talking about in Mr. Drabner's class? What's going on? Did he write you up?"

Mr. Drabner? Oh, right. Dribble's real name. I always forget. I shrug. "I'm *so* sorry. I don't know what I was thinking or saying. I haven't been feeling too hot. But Dribble was kind of cool about the whole deal. I mean, he didn't even give me detention or anything."

For some reason, Olivia gives me her small, crooked-teeth smile. "What did I do? Tell me what I said. I knew I was magic. Last night, I had a dream I was soaring, Erneski, on an orange moonpie rocket through firefly winks to you." She whirls around and smiles blissfully. Suddenly, I want to make like a spaceship and take off, but I keep myself grounded.

"Um, yeah, that's it. Olivia. You're so very powerful. Now, use your powers and tell me where Winslow might be."

She bites her lip and her eyes grow big and suddenly a little bit mean. "Winslow who?"

"Fromes. Is there any other Winslow in this school?"

She stamps a *National Geographic* about pregnant pygmies. The date thingie pounds right on the little woman's tummy.

"Have you seen him?"

"Nyet." Olivia keeps stamping, even though there's no more magazines. There's a reason, I think, that a female geek like Olivia, who happens to have very good bone structure, is a geek and not a diva. She has *zero* social skills. Can you imagine if teachers gave out grades for social skills? Then all of the geeks would fall to the bottom of the class.

"Do you know where Winslow would be?" I ask in a louder voice.

"Do I look like his mother? Dial 411 if you're so curious." Wow, Olivia has more attitude than me. She's done a complete one-eighty.

"I just thought that—"

"I'd be keeping track of him every sec because that's what I do with my time?"

"Something like that," I said. "It's a homework question."

She pauses, knotting her babushka scarf around her neck. "He's in the computer lab." I can't quite figure Olivia out. She's was just so nice to me, and then, with one mention of Winslow, she goes PMS.

As another student library aide rattles her book cart past me, I make a beeline for the computer lab. This is going to be easy-peasy pie.

Target Found

In the front of the room, I spot Winslow's big blond ponytailed head, which is sort of distinctly flat, like his mother put him down on his back too much when he was a baby. He's typing so fast the chain looped onto his pants clang against the chair. Today,

Winslow sports a white T-shirt with black spots that says *Deja Moo*.

I stand behind him and go, "Hey, Wins," in my best reel-in-a-boy voice, but he keeps on typing. Listening to their iPods, two girls next to him chat online with their friends.

"Heh-lo," I say again, stomping my foot. The girls turn around and stare. Winslow still doesn't budge. His thick fingers hip hop on the keyboard and his eyes laser into the screen, where a dragon shoots a ball of fire at a princess in a plunging-neckline–type dress.

As the princess sprinkles some dust, shrinking the dragon, Winslow mumbles, "Hey," to me, and then goes right back to staring at his screen filled with those flying dragons, centaurs, and scantily clad Xena types.

Is a computer screen *so* much more interesting than my face?

Yup. I, unfortunately, glimpse my reflection in the glass office next to the lab. My glasses don't fit—they are halfway down my nose. My hair makes a golden frizz halo around my shoulders. That's right—at the moment, I am Ernestine. This is *so* pathetic.

I tap Winslow on the shoulder. "I need to talk to you right away," I say urgently, and this time he turns around, blinking, as if the lights were just switched on after hours of darkness.

"Okaaaay," he says, obviously irritated at being interrupted. "What?"

The bell rings, blaring in my brain, and I realize a quiet moment alone in middle school is an oxymoron. *Where am I getting these vocab words from?*

"We'll walk and talk," I say. As the two iPod girls exit the computer lab, Winslow gathers up his messy binder, jams it into his canvas backpack, and I follow him out the door. As he weaves through the hallway, jocks bang into him, and he crashes into a kid in a wheelchair. His duct-taped shoes make a crinkly sound as he walks. Winslow is *so* oblivious. Can't he see everyone watching, disapproving? I can. They are also looking at me. Just being near him incriminates me further as a loser. As we stroll past rows of blue lockers, I can feel the stares. It's as if we're walking in a giant bubble together and every kid in the school wants to stick in a finger, see it pop, and watch the two of us disintegrate.

An Indecent Proposal

He's standing there with his ponytail, biting the ends of it. There's hair in his eyes, and a monster thrashing on his PDA. Warts dot the creature's face, and it blows smoke in my direction. Now the ponytail is out of his mouth and he's munching on some Cool Ranch tortilla chips.

"So, are you going?" I blurt out and nod over at a poster for the dance taped up on the cinder blocks above the water fountain.

"Where?"

"Winterfest. The dance."

Winslow shrugs. "What do you think?"

I don't. "Are you?"

He shifts his feet and cups his chin so that his neck cracks. He shrugs again.

"So are you?" I repeat, feeling all interrogator-like.

"Look at me," he says, patting his chest.

I take in his T-shirt, his ponytail, his duct-taped sneakers, and the smell of Cool Ranch tortilla chips.

"Do I look like the type of guy who's all, you know, psyched about going to the next middle school dance? Like, eeny meeny miny mo, which girl is it going to be this time because I'm such a hottie? Tell me. The truth, now. Do I look like that type of guy?"

"No," I say. "You don't." Why does the truth spurt out of my mouth at exactly the wrong time?

I'm much more comfortable repressing, exaggerating, and telling lies.

He flips the back of his ponytail like it's his finger. "Thought so." He plows past me and turns to go down the steps.

"You've got to go."

"Why?"

"Becaaaaaaaause"—for a moment I think about telling him the truth but this time, thankfully, I think better of it—"if you'll go, I'll dance with you!" I throw out my hands. "That's why."

"Oh, wow, that's so big of you."

"Winslow, it's not like that. Okay? Just show up. I'm telling you, I'm going. It's not a maybe. We—me and you—are *going* to dance at Winterfest. End of discussion."

"Yeah, yeah, whatever." He goes back to looking at the tentacled monster on his PDA. "Not my thing."

"You are so . . ." Ahhhh, I bite my tongue. Can I say what I *really* think of Winslow—I don't think so! Not again. "I'll dance with you. Are you getting this?"

"Look, I appreciate the effort but there're way too many people at one of those things. I've never gone to a dance and it's not like I'm going to start now. The whole thing's twisted anyway. Invented by Leadership girls to make the rest of us feel bad. That's sorta against my religion—being made to feel bad. I can do that on my own. Thank you very much."

"Okay, fine. Think whatever. But this is different. I'm not making you feel bad. I'm saying, Gooooooo. It'll be fun. We'll have fun. F-U-N. Fun."

"No." He shakes his head emphatically.

"No?!!" I'm getting mad now. REALLY MAD. WHAT. IS. HIS. PROBLEM??

"I don't think you like me," he says, sighing heavily.

I lean into him and smell his ranch-dressing breath. "What do you mean I don't *like* you?!!!"

He tugs on his ponytail. "Ever since sixth grade we've been, like, in competition—who's the biggest social loser. Me, gaming freak, or you—leader of brain girls. And some days, I win, and some days you're the big kahuna. But we've pretty much avoided each other, or I should say *you've* done that because, according to you, if the two of us were ever seen hanging out together it would be, what, like, double toxicity."

A bunch of stragglers blow past us in the hall

and, for the moment, we're sort of swept apart. I let them pass, and say, "I don't think that. I never thought anything like that."

He shuts his eyes and presses his fingers to his temples, as if the very thought of me gives him a major headache.

The second bell's going to ring any second. I *have* to get this over with. I don't think I can stand too much more of my new bizarro world. I lean even closer to him and see that his eyes are actually like Saturn—blue-gray with rings of yellow. "I like you, Winslow," I whisper. "Really. It's not that I'm happy about it. It's, like, weird because I don't want to like you because, look at you, I mean, I really do like you, though." I gaze at his lips, and they're full, fleshy, a little moist, and there was that love patch growing beneath it all, but I just have to do it—lean forward to kiss him, like with Justin on the swing at Petra's party.

Ohhhhhhh, How is this My Life?

I close my eyes because I can't look. Grasping with my arms, I reach out and pull him toward me, but it's not so easy because he's big and stiff as a board. I fall into him, into his canvas backpack with the little red buttons that say BYTE ME and DANGER, OPEN MIND, pressing into my ribs, and I start to kiss him. My lips graze his cheek, which feels cool and peach fuzzy. Puckering up, I search out his lips, still without actually opening my eyes, because I don't *actually* want to see what I'm doing on Winslow's face. I squeeze my stomach muscles together to avoid incoming nausea.

"Stop," commands Winslow, putting out his hand like a crossing guard. He sounds more than a *little* irritated.

I'm being pushed away. By Winslow?

In fact, I'm losing balance and falling onto the floor.

I peer up and see Petra and Caylin sashaying down the hall, and they are snort-laughing, which is NOT very becoming, even if you are beautiful. "Girl, did you just see that? Omigod," goes Petra, holding her stomach. "Ernestine's hot for Winslow."

Looking suddenly sheepish, Winslow shrugs. "It's not my fault. I'm a chick magnet. Can't keep 'em away." Then he glances at me like *I* am the one who wants to be Chewbacca's girlfriend. Hey, wait a minute. I sorta want to be Chewbacca's girlfriend. At least, I need to get him to the dance.

Sniggering, Petra bends down and stares at me. “Who’s next, Sneed?”

“I think it’s gonna be Mr. Dribble,” says Caylin. “She thinks his purple socks are hot.”

“It’s not what it looks like,” I say, standing up and brushing off my pants. Caylin and Petra make smooching noises all the way down the hallway. I CAN’T believe this. More whispers and giggles, strutting and turning back to stare at me.

Winslow leans down and glares. “I don’t know *what* that was about but *don’t* do it again.”

“Don’t worry, I won’t. Not a problem. Bloated computer nerds are not high on my to-kiss list. Whatever came over me was delusional.” *Uh-oh. Did I just say that?*

Winslow wipes his mouth with the back of his hand as if cooties are dancing on his lips. “That’s good because I’m more into human beings, you know, with feelings and normal human emotions. I guess you’ve got to do something desperate to get attention from a hottie such as myself.”

I want to kick him in his belly and rip away the bag of Cool Ranch tortilla chips from his doughy white hand. I want to shake him and tell that I am *not* ugly and desperate. HE IS! All of those e-mails to me, clogging up my pages on MySpace with his dumb comments. Those pathetic puppy-dog looks. That is gross. I am *not* gross. I have to do this. He didn't have to do any of that. "Can't you face up to reality?" I bellow. "Look in the mirror, dude." Why can't I shut up? My mouth is definitely not going to help me get Winslow to dance with me.

Winslow shuffles from me, disappearing in a new wave of kids hustling to make it to class before the second bell rings, and I feel relieved to be rid of him, but then Dribble passes me in the hallway and he's wearing his frowny face so that his bushy mustache curls into this upside down *U*. He's shaking his head at me. Omigod. I'm blowing this, big-time. What's my problem?

Simple

"I'll pay you," I say, catching up to Winslow and tugging on his ponytail.

"What?" He turns around. Was that a glare he just gave *moi*?

"Money. I'll pay you. Twenty-five bucks."

He puckers like I'm a human lemon and he's going to, like, spit out the seeds back at me.

"So what's your answer?" I ask him.

"What's the question?" he says.

"You know the question," I say through gritted teeth.

"Two hundred." His squints so that his eyes become slits.

"One hundred." Why do I feel like I've entered an eBay auction?

Suddenly, he smiles. "I've changed my mind. A thousand."

"A thousand dollars! Are you wacko? Where would I get that kind of money? In a week, maybe, I could get one babysitting job. Two tops."

He's moving away from me again. The second bell rings loudly, and you'd think they're warning us of an impending nuclear disaster. Winslow grimaces, and takes these giant steps with his clumsy clown feet down the hallway.

With my new, out-of-shape body, I huff, trying to keep up with him.

He looks at his digital *Star Wars* watch as everyone else races to get to their class.

"What? What could I do? I'll do anything. Winslow. Anee-thing. Okay. Just tell me. I'll do it. All right? Okay?"

"Anee-thing?" Winslow stops in his tracks and

peers at me like I'm the beginning of an alien infestation. The halls are about empty, except for some straggler skateboarder types, who look like they're still in a half-pipe.

"Yes, anything." I am starting to feel hopeful. He's taking the bait. Reel reel reel him in. That's my boy.

"Hmmmm, let's see here"—he taps his chin with the love patch—"you did just attack me, so maybe . . ." Winslow gazes into my eyes and I shudder.

Please. God. Love me. Shine your light on me at this moment.

Winslow, still deep gazing, pulls on one of the canvas shoulder straps of his backpack. "You're serious, aren't you? Okay, I want you to do the algebra homework for me for one week."

"Algebra? Are you kidding!" I hate algebra. I'd rather scrub the toilets. I'd rather fold clothes or . . . but it could be worse. Winslow could want me to get cozy with him. I can feel the oxygen come back into my body and I exhale deeply. There are worse things, right? "Just one week?"

"Yup. That's it." He hands me a ripped, stained assignment sheet on using the FOIL method to multiply two binomials, then turns the corner and slips into science class.

Ack. I'm Back.

As the bell rings, I sit down in one of the only seats left, which naturally is in the front row. Petra scowls at me. "What are *you* doing here?"

"It's called science class." I don't want to have to deal with this anymore. At least it's already sixth period, because I can't take another second of school or seeing my friends when I'm not me. And I certainly don't want to be looking over at Winslow, who's sitting in the back corner. But I can't help it. I do. I turn around and catch him, scanning his warrior-covered notebook. He doesn't glance up, or say hi, or give me a thumbs-up on our little math deal. Nope, he's deep in battle.

For a second, I scan the first problem in the stupid algebra homework:

The lesson on the distributive property explained how to multiply a monomial or a single term such as 7 by a binomial such as (3+8x). Use the FOIL method to multiply the following two binomials:

(24+8x)(5+2x)

For a moment, it all seems familiar. But that's crazy! I don't even understand what a monomial is in the first place. Mono, I know is a disease. Algebra is definitely one too. *Okay, calm down, Taf. One week.*

I can do this. One. Week. He didn't say the answers had to be perfect, right? He just said I had to do the homework.

I can feel someone pinching me. It's Petra. "Hello! This is *my* seat." She throws up her hands like a cross. "And don't start kissing me."

"Actually I'm Chewbacca's girlfriend. Don't have a fit." I get up. "I didn't see your name engraved on the desk."

Petra's brows lift and her lips form an *o*. "The geek's got attitude. Want some advice?"

"No," I say, sitting down in the desk across from her. "Not really."

Making smooching sounds, Petra grabs my backpack and slams it down on the ground so books and pencils clatter onto the floor. I'm not going to react. This is not my drama. Bending down, I stuff my binder and textbooks back into my backpack, and think about how Winslow just, like, twenty-four hours ago, was panting all over me.

Home Not Sweet

Sitting up in bed with pillows propped up against my headboard, I take a look at the algebra homework and I start to feel unbelievably drowsy. There is no cable

TV in this house to keep me awake, no DVR, and no Mom around. I am now falling asleep, even though it's only seven thirty. But that's okay, I tell myself as my head hits the pillow. I'll do it in the morning. And then it occurs to me. I didn't go to swim practice today, yet I'm still bone- and body-tired. Starting last year, I began swimming five days a week, with some weight training on Saturdays. Wow, I actually didn't go to swim practice today, and I don't need to go tomorrow.

I feel a little guilty about that.

Not really.

I'm a liar.

Parallel Universe

As I get to school, the bell is ringing to end social studies, which means somehow my alarm clock didn't go off and I slept until eight o'clock, which means I didn't have a chance to actually do the stupid algebra homework. For some reason, I thought I could get it done during social studies. Yeah, right. The more that I gaze at Winslow's sheet of algebra homework the more I know that I'm in deep. Brushing past the last group of students leaving Dribble's classroom, I hold up the algebra problems.

Dribble glances up from his desk, which is heaped with magazines, textbooks, and student papers he's dripped green pickle juice onto. He's reading *Time* magazine, the People section, and twirling his mustache. "Yes, ma'am. You wanted to talk?"

"Yes, I WANT to talk. Winslow did *not* want to dance with me, so I really can't help him. I mean, he's willing, but only if I do this!" I shove the math homework at Dribble.

He glances down at the assignment and pulls on his mustache. "Okaaaay."

"Winslow wants me to cheat for him, okay? I don't think that's the right thing to do. Do you?" Got ya. You're a teacher. What educator would be all, like, *Yeah, go ahead and cheat*?

He leans back in his chair and puts his feet on the desk, right onto a stack of graded papers. "Okaaaaay, if you think it's wrong. Then, there's your answer."

"It doesn't matter what I think. Right? You said I had to rectify. And get Winslow to dance with me. So if I want him to dance with me this is what I have to do—his algebra homework." Actually, it's also my algebra homework, but it's not like I've completely done that before either. It's hard to concentrate when a really good program is on TV, or a decent one, or a bad one.

Dribble stands up. "I've got a staff meeting, so if you'll excuse me, ma'am. It's time for your math class, isn't it?"

I bang my math book down on his desk. "This is insane. You have to do something."

He breaks into a huge grin so I can see his banana-colored teeth. "No, ma'am. I think it is *you* who has to do something."

Math Makes Me Sick

Outside of algebra class, I tell Winslow the bad news. He's standing in front of the water fountain completely oblivious that his huge form is blocking anyone from taking a drink. "I kind of got sick last night," I explain.

"Well, don't give it to me."

Folding his arms in front of the Milky Way galaxy on his T-shirt with an arrow that says YOU ARE HERE, he takes a side step away from me. The chain on his belt loop clangs against his leg. His duct-taped shoes squeak against the floor.

A clump of seventh-grade girls, their hands in their shoulder sacks, text away until a teacher passes.

I lean forward. "I just couldn't get to the homework. Okay?" I wave my hands in his face.

"What? But you . . . Oh, forget it." He looks like he's going to throw his big canvas backpack at me. "So you were really sick, huh?"

"Yes, very. I shouldn't even be in school, but my mom's a big believer in sharing whatever you have."

"Uh-huh," he says, moving farther away from me and almost banging into Petra and Caylin, who're discussing how lame somebody's outfit is. Mine, probably.

"Tomorrow. I swear. I'll make it up. You said a week. Just give me an extra day or something." The bell is ringing and now I'm the one sidestepping into Mrs. Grund's classroom. Now I'm actually feeling sick.

Before I know it, Mrs. Grund is making me sit at my desk and do math problems in class. I've always HATED math but I've always loved Mrs. Grund. If I close my eyes I can just see her ruffling her head of pink-blond hair, smiling at me, Petra, and Caylin and saying, "Oh, you girls. They put you to work all the time, I'm telling you. Go ahead. Sell your dance grams. But silently, okay?" She loves Leadership girls and lets them get out of doing EVERYTHING. Dance grams are a major La Cambia institution. They're these messages people buy for three dollars which Leadership posts up on the wall during dances, and EVERYBODY reads them. Mrs. Grund understands that. I mean, she might have a bad perm that makes her head look like a rose-colored dandelion, but she really gets it. But now, she's not letting me talk to my friends. Of course, right at the moment, I have no friends. I raise my hand and do the only thing I know will work with Mrs. Grund to get out of class. I tell her that I'm going to be sick. My life suddenly has a theme.

It's the Principal

"Who?" asks Mrs. Barnes, principal and mom of Caylin. She looks nothing like her daughter, though. While Caylin is perky, Mrs. Barnes lost perky long ago. She frosts her hair so it looks stripy and the beige foundation that she spreads on her entire face sparkles with sweat by midmorning. And she wears shirts that are too tight so she looks lumpy. But at least she doesn't wear pajamas. That's a leg up on my mom.

"You know, the social studies teacher, Mr. Dribble," I say. "No, I mean Mr. Drab."

"Mr. Drabner?"

"Yes, him." I shrug. "The kids all call him Dribble.

Because of the pickle juice and the spit that flies out of his mouth when he starts a rant."

"Look. If you're having issues, I'd be happy to have Mrs. Acorn"—she nods over at the secretary sitting behind the booth—"schedule an appointment with Mr. Ramirez." That would be the school counselor. The one for kids with problems.

"This isn't about me. It's about *him*. Mr. Dribble has . . . he's, well . . . magic. I think he has special powers."

"Uh-huh." Mrs. Barnes puts one end of her glasses into her mouth. I worry she's about to chew into the plastic and get poisoned. She mumbles, "Magic. Okay, keep going. As in tricks. Card tricks?"

"Real stuff. He . . . only uses it on special people he claims he wants to help."

"Okay. And you're one of the"—she makes little quotes—"'special people.'"

"I think. No, I know that. . . ."

She pops the glasses out of her mouth. "Have you been getting enough attention at home? Would you like more attention?" She eyes me, nodding and smiling at her cleverness.

This takes me by surprise. I notice there're a lot of books on her shelf about problem children:

the high-needs child, the explosive adolescent, the anxious one. Am I now one of these problem kids? Yup. As I stomp out of Mrs. Barnes's office I can hear her murmur to her secretary, "Definitely call the counselor; we have another kid with identity issues." You can say that again!

She's a Cheater?

I really have to go to the bathroom, so when nobody is looking I pop into the more-or-less off-limits faculty restroom.

While I'm in the stall, I hear the click of high heels on the tile floor. "So it's just an experiment, but I'm sure that if we test earlier it will make a difference," says a voice. A voice I recognize, a principal-ish voice.

Through the crack in the door, I spot Mrs. Barnes and she's on the cell phone to someone.

"Our scores have always been the highest in Menlo Park. Heck, better than Palo Alto. And that's saying a lot because all of the Stanford faculty brats. Yeah, I know. But what am I supposed to do with these guys? I mean, let's get real here." She's cradling the phone against her ear as she washes her hands in the sink. "Uh-huh, they're all English-language learners fresh from Oaxaca. And it's not fair to me that they're transferring them all into La Cambia. They're not even officially in the district. Yeah. Exactly. Totally. They're going to bring the scores down for the whole school. So if we test in January, when most of them are going to be Mexico then . . . perfect, right?" She yanks paper towels out of the dispenser so hard the thing rattles.

I pull my legs up on the stall. Somehow, I don't think that Mrs. Barnes would be too pleased to know that I am in here. I'm clearly not supposed to hear this convo. But I do know this much: It's really disgusting what's she's planning to do, treating ESL—English as a Second Language—students like they're some kind of super virus about to invade her school. Had Mrs. Barnes ever heard of Olivia Marquez? Hello. She might dress medievally, even Russian sometimes, but she's probably one of the smartest kids at the school. And her parents speak Spanish at home and probably go down to Mexico in January.

My heart hammers in my ears and throat.

What could I do with info like this? That my principal is planning on having the whole school cheat so she can look good. It is all about appearances and *not* about reality. It makes me sick.

For a moment, I think about flushing the toilet

and screaming, "I know you're going to cheat!" But I don't. I can't. After all, I was a cheater too.

I Want My Dada

Instead of copying whatever homework assignment is on the board, I pencil my name on the corner of the blank, ruled piece of paper in my binder. My *real* name. TAFFETA in big letters, and then, in a fit of paranoia that somebody has seen this, I begin erasing so vigorously that I rub a hole in the paper.

My English teacher, Ms. Stuckley, peers at me, her forehead wrinkling like a bulldog's. When she turns toward me, I want to laugh because she has a thing about her profile. In the yearbook, she only takes sideways photos, never full face on. I always imagined that it was because she wanted to be on money someday. Petra says it's because she knows only half of her is bearable to look at.

"Are you all right, Ernestine?" Ms. Stuckley asks in her pseudo English accent. "I am concerned about you."

Ms. Stuckley is worried about me? Language Arts diva, who snips, "Sit down," the moment I stroll into class? Ms. I-graduated-from-Wellesley-and-did-graduate-work-at-Oxford-so-I've-got-a-tattoo-of-C.S. Lewis-on-the-back-of-my-neck? Two days ago, the woman thought I was a complete bumblebrain. Her words.

Ms. Stuckley smiles, revealing her giant, rabbit-teeth overbite. "As I'm sure you all remember, last week everyone recited poems, four to six stanzas, using voice modulation, tone, and gestures expressively to enhance the meaning, and Olivia recited *Unda Canto*, which is a prime example of Dadaism. And since most of you all had no idea what Dadaism is, I wanted Ernestine to elaborate."

My lips move like I'm a fish trapped in a bowl.

"Gather your thoughts," says Ms. Stuckely, patting her close-cropped dark hair. "As I recall, you really provoked quite the debate."

Dadaism. What was that? I'm still working on the FOIL method.

I clear my throat to buy time and say, "I've really been hogging the convo, so I'd like someone else to have a chance to speak."

Score. Good save.

Ms. Stuckley's bottom lip droops down. "You're so generous, but please proceed." Winslow actually flickers a half a second of some real eye contact with me. I remember—could it only be a couple of days ago?—when he gave me such intense looks. It's weird but, in a funny kind of way, I almost miss it. He's only two seats away in the front row. It's like he's waiting for my answer. He won't talk to me outside of class unless I'm bribing him, but I can tell right now he's waiting for my words.

"I think da-daism is straight-up the best thing," I say, thrilled with my vagueness.

Ms. Stuckley taps the small gold earring by her left nostril.

"Because . . . ?"

For some reason, this thought flies into my brain: *Dadaism is the precursor to abstract painting and performance art. It started in Switzerland during World War I and focused on its antiwar stance by rejecting standards in art through anti-art cultural works.* Huh? What part of my brain is that?

I grip the eraser and dig into the sponginess with my nails. Dadaism. I know that. "Because Dadas are as important as Mamas, so it's wrong to be biased toward one parent. I love the Mamas and the Dadas' music, too!"

Everybody in the classroom laughs, especially Winslow.

"That, I assume, was a joke," says Ms. Stuckley, in a tight, pinched sort of voice.

"Yeah," I say, but inside I'm not feeling too jokey.

"Sounds like she needs a hint," says Winslow to the class. Great, Winslow thinks I'm ugly *and* dumb, a winning combination for any girl.

"So, class, you want to know what Dadaism is really?" says Ms. Stuckley, glaring right at me. "It's actually a cultural movement started in Zurich as an antiwar protest during World War I. Artists created works rejecting the standards of the time."

Whoa! Wow. That's what I was thinking in my head. Me! My brain! I actually knew the answer and even a little better than Ms. Stuckley. What else does Ernestine know? I'm starting to feel a little curious. Weird.

Phone Tag

When I get home, there's a message on the phone. I scroll through the caller ID numbers, and I see the familiar L.A. area code. Dad. I am pleased. It's Friday afternoon. A whole two days before Sunday, our day to talk.

I play the message. "What's up? It was good to hear your voice. You sounded upset and that had me all freaked. I can't wait to see you on your b-day.

I can't believe you're going to be the big one and four. You're making me feel old, girl. I gotta tell you about this TV show that we saw filming in Santa Monica. Reminded me of *Arrested Development* mixed with *Entourage*. You would have loved it, totally. Talk to ya lat-er."

Holding the rock that I picked up from our old yard as a souvenir, I call him back, but I get the machine and his voice mail on the cell. "Call me," I plead.

I can't believe it! We missed each other. On the counter, I spot a plate of nachos and pop a cheesy chip into my mouth and taste . . . meat. I haven't eaten meat in, like, six months and now I'm shoveling the chips into my mouth. I'm so hungry I can't stop eating. Maybe I want to get sick. And it's not like I need to worry about getting a cramp at swim practice because I don't have swim practice anymore. Ernestine apparently doesn't worry about keeping in shape.

Shoving another cheesy, meaty chip into my mouth, I glance over and see Mom, who is on the computer going over her most recent shots of the Culler twins in their Teletubby outfits. The desk space in front of her computer is littered with scraps of paper, pieces of chewed gum, bags of sesame sticks, various wrappers, pens, bills, and tissues. Behind the computer she has stacks of paper and notebooks filled with photos. There's so much mess, I didn't realize she was in the room. Usually, she's out doing her photography stuff. It feels so weird to have her here with me. I've gotten so used to being by myself after school that part of me feels really happy and the other part resents the intrusion.

I wait for the *I told you so*, but she doesn't say anything about Dad. I almost liked it better when she RANTED because it was like he was still around. Now, it's like he never existed at all.

If I divorce—but that SO won't happen because I'm going to make sure it's the real deal before I take the plunge—but if I do, and that's a big IF, I'll make sure to talk about my ex and have a couple of photos up, because it's not like he'd be dead or anything.

Just look at her. Mom clicks and scrolls using her latest Photoshop software. It's three thirty and she's still in PAJAMAS and hasn't run a brush through her hair. Can you blame Dad for leaving her for Big Lips, who was twenty-six and wore Juicy jeans? Not that he's with Big Lips now. But that's a whole other story.

Mom notices me for the first time, I think.

"How was school?" she asks.

"Good," I say. Would it do me any *good* to tell her the truth?

Prove It!

It's Sunday night, and I stare at the first problem in the algebra set and feel lost. I'm not sure what happened to Saturday. Spent it mostly hoping that my life would change back.

It didn't.

Did I ever figure out what FOIL stands for? No. Wait a minute. Friday, in Stuckley's class some part of part of my brain did know what Dadaism was . . . so maybe. Shutting my eyes, I sit quietly for a minute and . . .

NOTHING.

Except for what FOIL, in this case, isn't: something you use to wrap potatoes within the oven.

Getting something over on someone.

Then it comes to me! FOIL is an acronym, which stands for First, Outer, Inner, Last. The order that you multiply each grouping in the equation.

Could this be right? Do I actually know what I'm doing?

Petra is really good at math, but I can't exactly call her, and Mom uses a calculator for easy addition, and claims that anything with numbers flew out of her head years ago. And Dad. He's actually decent at math. But can I reach him? NO!

I hop onto the Web and look up the FOIL method and this site called Algebra Help.

> **FOIL** stands for: First—multiply the first term in each of the parentheses.
>
> Outer—multiply the outer term in each set of parentheses.
>
> Inner—multiply the inner term in each set of parentheses.
>
> Last—multiply the last term in each set of parentheses.

YES! YES! YES! My brain/Ernestine's brain was correct.

Although it isn't easy-peasy pie and I actually have to work hard, before I know it, I've conquered eight problems.

Time to E-mail

To: RunningDude@sbcglobal.net

From: Flipflop@yahoo.com

Dad,

Do you miss Napoleon as much as I do? I bet he would have loved being a beach dog down with you in

Santa Monica. Remember the time you, me, and Mom took him down to Ano Nuevo Point (and we had no idea it was elephant seal molting season)? Napoleon dashed up to us, with an elephant seal skin in his mouth, his swishy tail wagging, and I was spazzing because I thought the sweetest dog in the world had become a seal killer. Then we followed him to this corner, where there were literally a hundred elephant seals molting on the beach because it was June, and we all laughed so hard because those bulls weigh 5,000 pounds. There was just no way. . . .

I really miss Napoleon, and I MISS you so much. I still think it's so unfair that I can't go live with you down there.

Think about it, Dad. Pleeeeease talk to Mom, because my life right now EXTRA sucks and I can't wait to see you on my birthday weekend. Will you PLEASE!

Xoxo

Your daughter

I couldn't sign it Ernestine. Just couldn't.

Huh?

Dribble is writing on the board about the Constitutional Congress, but the first thing he writes is this: "This is only a glimpse."

The words sparkle, then he winks at me and

continues writing. I glance around the room to see if anyone sees the weirdness, but the rest of the class appears to be going about their regular lives of doodling in the margins of their lined notebook paper or, if you're Olivia, listening intently, as if she can't wait for another boring lecture on men in white wigs. You'd think if anyone could see sparkles, it would be Olivia.

I sit in the back of my class and stare at the chalkboard thinking about my life. A glimpse—glimpse of what?

A Glimpse

From the *American Heritage Dictionary of the English Language*:

> **glimpse** (glimps) *n.* 1. A brief, incomplete view or look. 2. Archaic. A brief flash of light. —glimpse *v.* glimpsed, glimpsing, glimpses —*tr.* to obtain a brief, incomplete view of. —intr. To look briefly; glance: *glimpsed at the headlines* [Middle English *glimpsen*. See ghel-2 in Appendix] **glims'er**, *n.*

Yes, it's all cleared up right now. I understand everything. Next thing that will probably happen is that world will stop spinning and everyone will fall off. Ha.

Actually, I do have hope. Implied in the word "glimpse" is the word "brief." Maybe this is like a forty-eight-hour thing, like a flu.

Erase Me!

Before algebra, the now-dreaded Mrs. Grund's class where I actually have to do math, I shove the homework at Winslow. "Here," I say.

He doesn't even say thank you. He just folds it and smashes it into his back pocket. One day down. Four more to go.

But then, suddenly, Winslow reaches into his pocket and scans the now-crumpled papers, nodding his head. His buddy Sneed lopes up next to him and murmurs. "Ernestine wrote Winslow a luuuuuuv note and he likes it." He begins howling with laughter, his cheeks blowing up like a trumpet player's.

"Idiot," says Winslow. "It's called algebra homework. See." He shows him the math sheet.

"But look at the way she forms her eights," says

Sneed. "Sexy!" Other outcasts, small geek boys I don't know the names of, crowd around and begin to bray like donkeys. I've apparently made their day.

Winslow. Winslow. Winslow. My life is going to be tortured by a chunky geek lord. I mosey down the hallway, feeling sorry for myself, thinking that I didn't even know the word "mosey" before . . . that only cows mosey, that I never used to eat cows . . . that I used to have a conscience about that, at least. What has happened to me???? AWWWWWHHGGGGG!!!!

What the Dickens?

The next period, Ms. Stuckley gazes at me like I'm the next poet laureate of America—as if I have already prepared brilliantly for our next assignment written up on the board in swirly cursive. This is all too much for a Monday morning.

Steps to Creating your Oral Report
Due: Tuesday, December 16

1. Interpret a book and provide insight. Select from the official 8th grade reading list.
2. Connect your own response to the writer 's techniques and specific textual references. This is imperative in delivering an oral response to literature.

3. Draw supported inferences on the effects of the literary work on its audience.
4. Support judgment through references to the text, other works, other authors, or personal knowledge. You may use visual aides in your presentations.

"Remember," says Ms. Stuckley, "I'm only giving you eight days for this assignment, so I suggest you use your time wiscly. Let's look at the steps on the board and get going." She peruses the room and listens to our groans. "Oh, stop wallowing in self-pity. Public speaking is one of the most useful skills you will walk out of here with. If you simply learn to stand up for yourself and speak your true voice, you'll have it made in the shade." Then she laughs as if she's a funny person.

It's hard to concentrate on Stuckley and her silly nose ring when all I'm thinking about is how I'm going to have to do more algebra homework for Winslow.

As Ms. Stuckley goes on and on about the virtues of oral literature and oral presentations gleaned from her days at Oxford, Ninai passes me a note.

I was worried about you on Friday in orchestra. Are you feeling better?

I look up from the note and give Ninai a thumbs-up.

If she only knew the real reason I was feeling sick. Suddenly, I'm realizing I can't hide out in the girls' room forever. I will have to figure out a more permanent way to get out of string class.

Then I get a note from Olivia.

Want to eat inside today?

Eat with Olivia and Ninai? How much longer must I continue this charade?

Hello. Wait a minute. Problem solved. Olivia, in addition to being a medieval Russian poet wench, is a math whiz, and Ninai probably isn't too bad herself. Not that I really need help, but it would be nice to check answers.

I mouth *yes* while Ms. Stuckley turns her back to write on the white board. It would be so MUCH easier to text. But apparently, Ernestine does not own a PDA.

Ninai smiles back at me and Olivia beams so hard that when she opens up her lips, I notice just how crooked her teeth are. (I bet as a medieval wench she's against anything as technologically advanced as braces.) Whether she's weird or not, I'm getting algebra answers checked from two certified brainiacs. I will be able to complete this stupid bargain with Winslow no problem now.

I feel like I've won something huge—like maybe a Hummer limo.

Welcome to Geekland

Petra and Caylin are tying Tyler and Justin's shoelaces together. Maggie the Mushroom and Invisible Girl look on enviously.

But I don't.

I'm not part of this anymore, not at the moment. I make my way through the crowded cafeteria over to Olivia, who's wearing her long peasant skirt today. Ninai is once again wearing her Girl Scout uniform. The whole khaki pants, white shirt with sash thing. You can tell she's proud that she has more patches or whatever than any other girl in troop 213. Olivia has a *Webster's Unabridged* in the middle of thc table—I think they use it to play dictionary games.

Olivia pats me on the shoulder. "Are you feeling better? Would you like some tea?" She points to a green thermos that looks like it's been around since the seventies. There is no way I would drink anything from that contaminated thing, but I don't want to be impolite. Olivia is seeming human. "Um, no thanks. My stomach's a little funny."

"Mangia, mangia!" Olivia flicks her hands at me like she's apprenticing to be Hermione Granger from *Harry Potter*. And she says it in a really loud voice. In fact, she's picked up her medieval writing device and is pointing it around the room. I can hear Justin, who's sitting next to Tyler, yell, "Are you fondling your pen again, Olivia?"

But Olivia doesn't seem to notice. In fact, she doesn't seem to care that the guys, I mean The Guys, are laughing at her, including Tyler I'm-beautiful-kidnapped-boy Hutchins. Petra is smirking.

I stare as Olivia swivels. "What exactly are you doing?"

"Making you feel better. I think you're right. About me. Having, you know, some sort of woo-woo powers." She peers at me, squinting her eyes witchily. "Do you feel a little bit better?" I can hear Petra's distinct laughter in the background.

"Um, a tiny bit," I say quietly, trying to butter her up and still not get noticed.

I Love Mathematics!

Olivia pulls out her bagged lunch, which looks to be straight from Trader Joe's—spring rolls, carrot sticks with a built-in ranch dip, and a PowerBar. "That must explain Friday. You were so lost in English. I loved it when you said that Dada was Mama's husband."

"So funny," says Ninai, giggling. What does the girl have to be happy about? She's at least thirty pounds overweight with giant paws for hands.

"Yeah, well," I say, doing what I do best: making excuses. "It's the cold medication. Like you said, I'm not myself." I pick at my egg salad sandwich. "I'm feeling weird and I was totally hoping you could help me out with some of the algebra homework," I say as casually as possible.

Ninai raises her eyebrows, and so does Olivia. "Why would *you* need help?"

"It's because I really love math, and I feel I've been taking my methods for getting answers for granted when using that FOIL thingie, and want to find out how you girls do it. Some quality sharing time on the subject I love best." And then I start to giggle because the idea of me actually loving math, actually wanting to do more of it is SO RIDICULOUS. But I can't be giggling about this right now. I need to be serious, so I turn my snorts into something that I hope sounds like a pathetic sob. "Maybe the problem is that I used to do my homework to the TV since Mom stays up very late working on her photography stuff. I hardly see her. And it creeps me out, so that's why I turn it on and sometimes I start actually watching instead of using it for background noise. The truth is I live in panic."

"You do?" Ninai looks at me with a baffled expression on her face. I think I'm giving away too much information but for some reason I can't stop further blurtation.

"Yes, we had a DVR but Mom stopped payment on that and cable so I basically now only have an iPod to keep me company. It's so annoying. Because she's not the one all by herself. She wants us to get DVDs, but on the weekend only."

"Couldn't you get downloads or something?" asks Ninai.

I shrug. "Maybe. It's not the same. My computer screen is so little. It'd be annoying."

Olivia peers at me all squinty-eyed, like she's trying to be a therapist. "Okay, so it sounds like you're actually upset about being by yourself."

"Um, yeah. I guess. Can we move on to another subject? Like will you guys help me?"

Ninai grabs my arm. "Sure, I don't see why not."

"I can cast some math spells," says Olivia, nudging the thermos of tea over to me. "I think this brew will give you a whole new way of looking at equations."

"You know I'm serious, right?" I ask, biting my bottom lip.

"Yes," says Ninai, grabbing her binder. "For number one I got seventeen. What did you get, Ern?"

Glancing at my math book opened to page 123 on my lap, I see paragraphs upon paragraphs talking about inners and outer terms, and all of it is making sense.

So when Olivia asks if I want to work on algebra with them and compare answers, I say yes!

This time I take the tea. Olivia and Ninai scoot their chairs closer to me and we get to work. Olivia keeps on talking about first terms and outer terms and then inners and outers like we're talking about belly buttons. I'm talking inners and outers back and actually liking it.

After it's over, my head is filled with numbers, *x*s and *y*s. I say, "Thank you. That was fun," and I'm feeling like maybe I'm beginning to understand Ernestine's brain.

Olivia sips her tea. "I was just about to ask you what you thought of *The Unicorn's Revenge* because

I didn't get why L'Nere would transform from the other realm."

"*The Unicorn's Revenge*? Um, am I reading that?" I ask.

"Reading that? You can be so funny sometimes. *You* said you wanted to start a unicorn club!"

Did I say I was beginning to understand Ernestine's brain? Maybe not.

Like, for Real!

One problem solved. Orchestra. I write a note in illegible doctor-y handwriting from Gerald Schlesinger, MD, saying I need to be excused from orchestra rehearsal because of tendonitis in my elbow. Brill! Because Mr. T buys it. Double brill because I say I need to use fifth period to go to physical therapy. He swallows that whopper too.

Now I'm thinking about actually entering the medical profession. Think how useful it could be for your life. You could write your own excuse notes. Like, for real!

Bad Monkey

"Here," I say, holding the math homework above Winslow's ponytailed head, as he reads some fantasy novel involving a sword-wielding goat man.

Lazily, he raises his chin, squinting as if trying to figure out exactly who I am. His T-shirt, which has a picture of Curious George that says BAD MONKEY, has little orange and green flecks on the bottom like he's been wiping his hand on it after eating too many Cool Ranch tortilla chips. Suddenly, he seizes the paper that I'm so proudly clutching in my hand and slaps it down in front of him, glances at it, nods, then stuffs it into his canvas backpack without so much as a *merci*. I'm so happy to have gotten through this first hurdle that I practically bounce back through the cafeteria to Olivia and Ninai. I have handed in my second round of math homework to Dungeon Master Winslow Fromes.

No Free Lunch

I gaze down at Olivia, who's furiously scribbling in her journal, her long, hennaed hair curtaining her face so it seems impossible that she can actually see a thing. But I notice she writes in perfectly neat capital letters that amaze me with their exactness. Her flowy peasant dress with bells on the sleeves chimes as she moves her hand. I'm feeling so grateful that I'm getting math that I can't contain myself. "That dress is a-mazing. I mean it. It looks so good! Incredible. It's, like, the best dress. Did you hear me? The *best* dress I've ever seen at this school?" I say. So it's gauzy and tentlike—but I never noticed before how the swirls are quirky and fun. And the bells are even a little cool if you're into a belly dancing–type atmosphere.

Olivia carefully puts down what looks like a black fountain pen, caps it, and then bites into her giant turkey sandwich.

"Smells delish-ious," I say pleasantly, even though it smells gross and meatlike.

Huffily, Olivia scoots back her chair and turns away from me. "What's with her?" I ask Ninai.

"I think you know," she says.

"I do?"

"Winslow Fromes. Ringing any bells for you now?" I want to laugh at the bell reference because the chimes on Olivia's sleeves are chiming. She picks back up her cloth-covered journal to start writing.

Suddenly, it hits me. That's why Olivia was acting so weird in the library that day. SHE'S CRUSHING ON WINSLOW! When I just dropped off the algebra homework in the cafeteria, she thought I was scoping her man!

"Olivia, don't be crazy. I . . . I don't like Winslow."

I try to think of a very good reason that I would've been whispering in his ear conspiratorially in the middle of the La Cambia cafeteria. "The reason I was with Winslow just now was I thought I could help you out. You know, talk you up. Since the Winterfest is coming up in eleven days." Not that I'm counting. Yeah, right.

Olivia scribbles furiously into the purple journal, and turns to hold it up for me to read:

Ostrich down. Feathers up.
Head. Sand. It's what I see.
But do you see me?

"Huh?" I say. Is it that I don't get poetry or that I don't get Olivia?

"Zdrashdrapke kak dela," she mutters under her breath.

Olivia bites her lip and madly swings her long, stringy hair out of her watery eyes. "It should be obvious how I feel. And Winslow should see that, and come to me. I don't need your help unless I ask for it, but"—she hesitates—"I appreciate your effort, you silly billy." My heart balloons with gratitude. I think the poet wench has forgiven me.

"But how would Winslow know how you feel, since you hardly talk to him?" I ask.

"I would if he'd approach me." She actually puts her hand over her heart. "Maybe I'll cast a love spell on him and change his name to Boris. That's what I call him."

"All you have to do is get close to him but, like, in a flirty way. A little accidental epidermis contact, you know?"

Olivia scrunches her forehead so her eyes almost clamp together.

"Just grab his palm and start reading his fortune," I suggest. "And then make little light swirling motions with your fingertips. I know W-i-n-s-l-o-w would so love it."

I hear Olivia groan and she turns away from me, with a look of utter disgust. As if she's Shakespeare and I'm the *National Enquirer*. "Stuff like that works. I'm serious. I know someone who flirted like that *all* of the time and Winslow once asked her to Winterfest."

Hands on her hips, Olivia flares her nostrils. "Like who?"

Like Taffeta, I think. I come so close to shouting it, but instead bite down on my lip.

"Who did Winslow ask to Winterfest?" insists Olivia.

"I can't remember exactly," I say. "It's one of those cutesy, freaky, made-up names."

"That's because she doesn't exist," states Olivia, pushing her hair out of her eyes.

I go to open my mouth to protest, but I don't. I can't. Because Olivia is right. She doesn't exist.

More 411

I see Winslow clomping down the hallway, his canvas bag stuttering on his shoulder, his chain on his belt loop clanking. Checking left and right, I make sure there's no Olivia creeping behind me in the corridor. Running over, I plant myself in front of Winslow so that he'll ACTUALLY see me. "Look, I can't be giving you the algebra homework in the cafeteria like that again," I say. Not adding *because if Olivia sees me all tête-à-tête with you she'll definitely throw a medieval Russian fit.*

Winslow bows his head so that his ponytail flops over his shoulder. He says, "I totally agree, it's not the best locale," which completely surprises me. I thought he didn't care what ANYONE thought about him. "Next time, why don't you give it to me before sixth period during the fifteen-minute break?"

"Works for me," I say, as he gives me a lopsided

grin. Then, like a magnet, Olivia draws toward us, and, just in time, I duck and run for the cover of the girls' room.

The Ride

"Ernestine, I'm not driving you!" Mom calls out from her bedroom. I can hear her munching on sesame sticks. For breakfast, I'm surprised she doesn't put them in her cereal bowl with some milk.

"Mom, pleeeeeease. I've been up all night doing algebra with Olivia. And when I stay up all night, I mean it. No sleep. Lots of Reese's Pieces to keep me awake." Of course, Dad wanted to talk last night too. Of all times. I spoke with him for, like, three minutes because I was going through all the bookshelves in the apartment trying to figure out what book I want to pick for my oral report. Can this really be moi? The things's not due for a week. I really am such a geek now.

Mom glances at the clock. "Honey, the Realtor's meeting me here at the apartment in ten minutes to sign some house-sale papers. It never ends. You have your pajamas on," she says, almost laughing as I pass by her room.

Was I actually going to go to school in my pink

floral flannel pajama bottoms? That's so sick. Running upstairs, I pull out a pair of jeans and a T-shirt and put them on. Mom peeks her head out of her bedroom. "Your shirt's on backward," she says, smiling.

Okay—when did I become a clone of my mom?

So I bike to school on Mom's bicycle built for two because the chain on my bike fell off as soon as I tried it. Me pedal to school on Mom's dinosaur? Who woulda thunk? But, you know, I am tired of not doing anything physical. And even though, solo, I look ridiculous, I don't care because it's not like anyone knows me, exactly.

Dribble Dribbles

Before I have a moment to recover, Dribble hobbles toward me with this bogus concerned look on his face. "How's it going?" he asks.

"Are you serious? How's it going? Like, la la, just another day? It sucks, that's how it's going."

He shrugs and his orange mustache seesaws. "Okay, anyhoo, just checking in."

"Checking in? How can you be so casual? Because you're making me look, feel, and act INSANE!"

As a student approaches his desk, Dribble shifts his gaze and glares at me. "If you continue to use that tone of voice, young lady, I'll have to write you up."

Write you up? He's the one who should be written up. Giant warnings blasted all across the state. The country. THE UNIVERSE!

He leans into me and I can smell pickles. "Sorry. Need to act like a teacher around"—he lowers his voice—"the others."

"So you're implying you're not a teacher?" I blurt.

"And you're not Ernestine," he says in a low voice.

"You're so . . ."

"Frustrated. I can see you most certainly are." He bangs down on his desk. "Don't give up. Keep your eyes on the prize. Remember what you really want, because things are going to get ugly."

"Thanks for the pep talk. You're *so* helpful." Not.

"Anytime, Ms. Smith." As I walk away, he's chomping on a pickle, of course. Maybe he's pregnant or something.

Stepping Up

In algebra, a roll of toilet paper smacks the back of Olivia's head.

Mrs. Grund whips around and peers at the class. “Okay, who did it?”

Of course, nobody raises their hand. I mean there are some dumb kids at La Cambia but not THAT dumb.

“I did it,” I overhear Petra whisper to Invisible Girl who sits in front of her. She’s that friend of Maggie the Mushroom. “I wanted to draw attention to Olivia because she looked SO beautiful today.”

“I heard what you said, Petra. And it makes me mad.” I know my voice is rising but I can’t help it. I lean into her. “Do you know what that’s called, Petra? Projection. You must think you’re *not* so beautiful today. Maybe your five-foot-two mother called you an Amazon again because she didn’t sell a house so she’s afraid she can’t make the Lexus payments since your dad is an embezzler. Or maybe Caylin is ignoring you. We all know the only reason she keeps you around is to be her bodyguard.”

Petra gives me her best withering death stare. Meanwhile, Olivia leans over my desk and murmurs, “Thank you.” And when she says you—and means me—I feel like she means me for the first time.

Blahh!

As the bell rings for fifth period, Ninai catches up to me in the hallway in the music building. "Mr. Takashama wants us to really go over the second movement of the concerto. Does that sound good, Ms. Soloist?"

No, that does not. I'm planning on spending fifth period in the bathroom again. And I've got that doctor's excuse note, thank you!

Then Mr. Takashama pops his head out into the hallway. "Great, you're back."

I shake my head and pat my elbow. "Still hurting."

"But you're not in therapy today." He smiles at me. "That must mean something."

Yes, that means I'm busted. "There was a cancellation," I explain so he doesn't think I'll be in class tomorrow.

He shrugs. "I think we need to talk to your mother about scheduling these appointments after school." He grabs his cell phone and flips it open. "Want me to call?"

Chill, Taffeta. Don't let him see you sweat. "No worries," I say, smiling. "It was just a weeklong therapy sort of thing. With this specialist guy. But I'm done with that, so no need to bother my mom at work."

"I'm glad to know that you're back," he says, putting down his phone. "Sure you can't play today?"

"Maybe soon."

"But you *can* sit down with us." He opens up the doors to the orchestra room and ushers me inside.

Blahh. Looks like I'm going to have to *actually* sit through orchestra today.

Special Delivery

I amble into the library after fifth period to give Winslow his homework when I see Olivia stamping *Seventeen* magazines. What is she doing here? Oh, right. Olivia has library skills for her elective. Olivia spots me, so I shuffle over to the desk as she grabs a stack of books taller than the Eiffel Tower and shoves them onto a shelf. "What's up?" I ask.

"I am ready now to use my powers on Winslow." She gives her big crooked-tooth smile.

"Okaaaay." Suddenly, I'm feeling guilty. I'm picturing Olivia watching me dancing with Winslow at Winterfest.

"I'm going to focus on Winslow for real. I think if I just concentrate and, you know"—she squints and flicks her fingers—"la mangia wahza doolia!" The stack of *Seventeen* magazines on her desk drop with a loud thud onto the tile floor, nearly crushing a potted plant. "Whoops, I felt that. Did you? All of this energy moving."

"Well, some magazines did move," I admit.

"In the hallway yesterday, I was thinking about Winslow, and then, poof, he appeared at the water fountain. I think I called him to me telepathically. So maybe"—her eyes sparkle—"I'll telepathically invite him to Winterfest, too." Olivia starts swaying her hips and singing high and off-key, "We'll make magic on the dance floor." She's apparently out of touch with reality *and* with her vocal range.

I'm grabbing the magazines and stacking them back neatly, spine out, and saying very quietly, "That's a brilliant idea, Liv. I'm sure it'll work. But maybe you ought to try, you know, regular flirting with him too."

She tilts her head to gaze at me. "I'm not so sure. But stranger things have happened."

Yes, I think, as I start backing up. Stranger things *have* happened. "Well, I've got to go into the computer lab and figure out what I'm doing for my oral report thingie, but keep on working on your powers." I walk backward into the computer room, glad to be rid of her so I can finally give Winslow some more homework. Wouldn't it be nice if I could telepathically give it to him?

Frantic Phone Call

I can't believe I'm back at my so-called home, having to think about algebra *again*. Mom's out working on a special project for her photography class on the metamorphosis of Main Street. So far she's photographed cement trash cans in front of Rite Aid and a McDonald's in East Palo Alto and then the JZ Cool Eatery on Santa Cruz Avenue. Of course her medium, Tosh, suggested this brilliant trash-can idea and she actually asked if I wanted to come with her. For some reason, she thought me learning how to shoot trash would be educational. Ha. It was because she needed someone to lug around all of that heavy equipment. That's why. She even tried to sweeten the deal with promises that we could later play around on Photoshop together. As if, even without having swim practice these days, I have time to mess around on the computer when I have to pay attention to stupid algebra EVERY DAY!

My desk is my bed because apparently there isn't enough room in my bedroom for an actual desk. My back hurts, even though I've got pillows propped up against the backboard as I flip through my algebra book. Numbers are SO annoying because they are always the same. I think they would be much more interesting if you could accessorize them, say with a purse, or cool pair of heels from Marc Jacobs.

Olivia and Ninai, SOS! I IM them. I need help on this algebra homework and I'm thinking about going on a bike ride so I ask if they'd like to join me. The truth is I'm almost thinking that I don't need their help, but then I'd be all by myself thinking about numbers. And I hate being alone with numbers. And, even more than that, I hate being alone with me.

Freedom. Not!

Another day of surviving, of seeing Dribble and knowing that he knows but won't do anything about it. Leaving me all alone to do important things like count the cracks in the tile floor and listen to him drone on about an important unit test coming up in five days, on December 15 (four days before my birthday and Winterfest). Something about the Constitution and the founding of the United States and letting freedom ring. I'm not exactly relating to freedom right now, Mr. Dribble. I'm fighting my own Revolutionary War. Maybe I could write an authentic essay and tell the world about my life, Mr. Dribble; would that count for a grade?

Not My Favorite Facility These Days

After algebra, I'm standing by the sink that won't stop running when The Girls file into the bathroom. They squint at me, smirking in their knowing way. I glance at them with their tight jeans, flip-flops, smooth, silky hair, big teeth, and chatter. They give off a certain energy, as if everything fantastic in the universe swirls around only them, and if you're not them, life's a black hole.

They chat like they're all psyched about the limo they'll be taking to Winterfest. How could they be talking about the limo?—my idea, for my birthday! "It'll be sooooo cool," I hear Caylin say, her voice all enthusiastic, as she leans forward in the mirror, reapplying lip gloss.

"I bet it'll have a refrigerator," says Petra, "With an endless supply of soda and energy drinks."

"Hey, wouldn't it be fun if we all matched? The color of the limo, I mean," says Caylin.

"Ew, bad idea," I say, committing instant blurtation. "That'll be, like, over the top."

Petra's chin drops and her lower lip sags. I think I can see her tonsils. But she recovers and says, "Who asked you, freak?"

"I guess not you," I say. "I was just listening to you, or whatever."

Caylin wrinkles her nose and shakes her head at me. She does this when she feels sorry for someone.

I ache to tell Caylin that doing favors for Winslow is BEYOND awful. The very thought of it makes my stomach clench. I mean, really, to have to work so hard to get his attention feels unnatural. Besides, if I get too close to him I might not be able to resist tearing that silly little wannabe soul patch off his lower lip and cutting off that unkempt ponytail.

Strange and Mysterious

As Ms. Stuckley allows us to work on organizing our oral presentations, I stare at the book I've chosen, *Oliver Twist*. At first, I chose it because I've seen the musical and wouldn't have to read the book, but it's actually pretty short and even exciting so, despite my best intentions, I'm really reading it. Weird.

When I look over at Caylin turning the pages of *Holes,* I don't feel jealous (I'd wanted that one because I had seen *that* movie, too). Weirder.

Sick of It

"Sick again?" says Mr. Takashama, shaking his floppy hair in a gesture that looks like he's auditioning to play in a Beatles tribute band. "Oh, Ernestine," he sighs, scratching the back of his head. "Noooooo. And right before the concert, too."

I can feel every red blood cell draining from my circulatory system. I need to get out of here for so many reasons.

"Wowee," says Mr. Takashama. "You aren't yourself, are you?" I don't know how to best and most accurately answer that question.

Yes, you're right, Mr. T, I'm not myself. I'm a completely different person or I appear to be in a parallel universe, Mr. T. Me. But a different version of me, as if I had made different choices. A fresh start. Or, if you look at my complexion, I would say a stale start. Sounds familiar? Sounds insane, Mr. T? That's okay, because that's exactly how I'm feeling at the moment.

Special Delivery #3

I pull out *Seventeen* magazine and flop down in a library chair, stretching out my legs. Delivering homework to Winslow can wait a second. I flip through the fashion section, and then peruse the articles.

Suddenly, I am sensing someone sitting next to me. A male, breathing or wheezing through his nose in a way that screams, *I regularly use an inhaler*.

Yes, it's Winslow, holding a can of chocolate Yoo-hoo. Why does he have to come the minute I'm reading "10 New Ways to Flirt with Your Guy"?

Immediately, idiotically, I spread my hands over the article so he can't read what I'm looking at. My life is SO annoying.

He snort-laughs and slaps the back of the chair like it's a poker buddy. "Can I try that too?" he asks, splaying his hands next to mine over the article. "Wow, it worked. See, we are flirting, *ma chérie*."

I can feel myself turning red. He is *such* a pain. I close the magazine and throw it on top of the rack. "Here," I say, handing him the algebra homework. "I think I've pretty much nailed these. It was SO EASY. The whole multiplying each term in the left polynomial by the entire second polynomial and using the distributive property to simplify the thing."

Wow. I'm sounding math-smart. I *am* math-smart.

For a moment, his eyes leave his notebook and scan the problem sets. "Yeah, they're fine."

He pulls out his binder, and I glimpse the warrior-covered notebook. I have the urge to snatch it and flip through the pages, but I don't. Instead, blurtation, "You ever notice how Ms. Stuckley always has her photo in the yearbook in profile?"

Winslow closes his eyes and thinks a moment. "Yeah. That's right."

"What's up with that?"

"I dunno." Winslow shrugs, and Einstein, who's featured on his T-shirt today with a thought bubble that says IMAGINATION IS MORE IMPORTANT THAN KNOWLEDGE, appears to wink at me. "Maybe on one side where she's got her nose ring she's covering up a big wart."

"Or she imagines herself on"—I flip a penny out of my pocket—"on money. Replacing Abe maybe."

He starts to laugh and I'm noticing this man and woman on Winslow's PDA screen saver. They look like the kind of super good-looking young couple in love you'd expect to see on the little piece of paper that comes with a frame. "And why do you have that?" I ask, trying to figure out who they could be.

"Oh, *them*," says Winslow. "My parents. An old

photo from before I was born. My mom put it there yesterday because I was asking whether Dad was born with his beard because I've never seen him clean-shaven, so she put this on my PDA."

"Oh," I say, completely baffled. "I didn't think somehow . . . ," I flick my eyes at Winslow.

"That'd they'd be normal-looking?"

"Um, yeah."

"Trust me. They're not. Sometimes I'm not sure my dad can see me. Thick glasses. Like this." He spreads his hands apart six inches.

My jaw must be dropping because Winslow laughs.

"I'm kidding. He's got twenty-twenty vision. My dad's a pretty cool guy. Just quiet, actually. Not a big talker. I'm more like my mom in that way. But my dad is a big guy. Most people look at him and wouldn't go, 'SLAC shooting particles down a mile-long tube.' They'd go, 'coach' or something. Except for the thick glasses."

"I thought you said he doesn't wear them."

"He doesn't. I just wanted to see if you were paying attention." He jabs me on the shoulder. "But the SLAC part is real."

Slack? Sounds like me as a student. Okay, I can't

stand it anymore. I have to ask. "Uh, what's 'slack'?"

Winslow shakes his head. "Where have you been? It's right on Sandhill. The Stanford Linear Accelerator Center? Internationally famous, at least among science geeks. A mile-long underground tube for people who like to shoot subatomic particles—we're talking a *very* expensive toy. My dad finds it much more interesting than his family. I would too, if I were him."

"What about your mom?" I ask.

He lowers his voice. "This is going to sound sick. But she's pretty hot, actually."

"You have a hot mom?"

"And sister. She's a sophomore at Cal. Yeah. Sorry to say. It's kind of weird when my friends say it. My mom's really beautiful and smart, and on me all of the time about how much time I spend on the computer playing my game. Which is SO funny since she makes money off of people like me who are obsessed with computers. She works for a high-tech venture capital fund. She's a math head. Just more corporate than my dad. My dad basically lets her rule and redo the house as long as he gets to spend time underground at SLAC."

I'm pondering this, putting together this really sophisticated woman and thinking *This is her son*? She looks like the kind of mom I'd want to have. One who cared about how she looked. One who might actually take me to the Stanford Mall and buy me things. "Doesn't your mom care about you? I mean, you write all over your jeans. You wear a chain. Duct-taped shoes. Doesn't this bother her?"

Winslow pulls on the little hairs on his chin. "No, I think it reminds her of my dad. She's into geniuses."

"So you're saying you're a genius." I sit, taking in his big, goofy smile.

"That's it. I'm a genius," he says in a singsongy voice. "You're right, for once!"

I throw a *PC World* at him that's conveniently hanging on the wooden rack in front of me.

Winslow stands in front of me, squaring off.

I pick up a green cushion from the nearby couch and hold it over my head.

He picks up the other cushion and holds it over his head.

I whack him over the head. He whacks me back. The cushions tear apart as we slam each other. Pieces of yellow foam fly everywhere. A fern knocks over and dirt spills onto my shirt. "Now I smell like mud.

You are *so* dead." I grab Winslow's opened Yoo-hoo and fling it into his face. But the boy ducks!

He opens up another one and dumps it over my shirt.

As bits of chocolate soda drip down onto my shoes, he grins. "Now you smell much better."

The Notebook

Winslow leaves, but not his backpack. With all of the Yoo-hoo flinging, he forgot it somehow. This leaves the perfect opportunity to look at that dragon-covered notebook. Quickly, I unbuckle the canvas bag and slip it out. The blood pounds through my center. What could possibly be in there? When I crack open the book, I see nonsense words that mean NOTHING to me. Here's an example:

Two, eight, eight
Kibon
Taegeuk
Palge
Everything changing
No end

Not Me!

Olivia is raging on the phone to me and Ninai. "You should have seen the library. The cushions on the green couch were completely ripped apart. You know, the ones by the magazine rack. And chocolate milk was EVERYWHERE! Not a pretty sight."

"Yuck," says Ninai, groaning into the phone.

"Yeah, who would do something like that?" I ask, feigning total horror and disgust. I'm such a skilled liar. Could I make a career out of this?

Double Dribble

In Dribble's class, there is no one for me to talk to because Olivia and Ninai actually take notes, so I'm finding that there is nothing left for me to do but pay attention to Dribble. "Listen up, people," he intones. "Four more days until your test on the Constitutional Congress." He waggles his puffy mustache. "So I heartily suggest you remember in all of your weekend socializing to set aside some study hours. Got it?"

I get it, Dribble. The whole thing. And it's scaring me.

More Delusions

Before algebra, I could swear that Petra winked at Winslow in the hallway. The likelihood of this would be the equivalent of me waking up tomorrow morning with a chest the size of bowling balls. Then Mrs. Grund actually compliments me on my homework. This feels very strange because in the past she complimented me on my jeans or fabulous hair, which nobody can figure out the color of. (It's reddish blond—no, blondish red or brownish blondish red) and my ability to sell dance grams. And then I think about how in all of these algebra problems they're always using *x*, so I started to wonder why *x* and so I actually raise my hand to ask Mrs. Grund. "Why *x*?" I ask.

"Why not," she answers.

The Big Drip!

Ms. Stuckley reminds us in her pseudo English voice that "our eagerly awaited oral presentations are due on Tuesday, December sixteenth. Five more days to polish." Then she intones, "Please get out the book that you are working on, so I can go around the classroom to visit each one of you for an update on how your oral report is coming along." I start to open up *Oliver Twist*, but then I bolt to borrow the bathroom pass because I REALLY have to go.

But who should be coming in when I'm going out the door, who isn't even in Ms. Stuckley's class?

Tyler, freaking-I'm-so-beautiful-I-could-just blind-you-with-the-sum-combination-of-my-white-teeth-green-hair-and-general-swimmer-boy-buffness. That's who. Tyler who escaped from kidnappers, that's who.

I try to edge around him but he stops me and goes, "Hey."

Just like that. "Hey" to me now. In this form, with the stupid giant bathroom pass in my stupid hand that is attached to my body. I can't help it. To revive myself, I take in his kidnapped-boy scent. Today, he's all chlorine and mint.

"Hey," I say back.

"Is this, like, Ms. Stuckley's room?" he asks, barely moving his mouth when he talks. I think that is SO cool. It's like he's already in training to be made into a statue, like Michelangelo's *David*.

He's looking down at my right hand, which is not exactly covering over the length of the jumbo-size wooden bathroom pass because you can definitely see where it is carved in black letters—BATHROOM PASS. It might as well be written I NEED TO PEE.

As I try not to bounce in place, Tyler's eyes flick over at the pass.

Why me? Why do you have to look there now? You barely move your mouth, do you have to move your eyeballs and lock on to the piece of wood that lets you know that I have to either go number one or number two—and am holding the most embarrassing piece of wood ever? It's bad enough that my name is Ernestine and I have frizz head, but this means that you, Tyler, eighth-grade god, know that I need to relieve myself at this very *moment.*

My hand clamps down on the wooden pass and with my other hand I make a fist and cover the rest of the pass, like I am riding a bicycle. Or waterskiing. Waterskiing is sexy. Yes, I'm a brilliant waterskier on holiday.

Vacations are sexy, especially near large bodies of water.

I, Ernestine, at this moment am sexy.

Tyler flicks his shamrock-green eyes at me. "Well, looks like you better get going."

"Yeah, probably." I shrug. "No worries."

Then I'm hearing heavy, sloppy, slouchy footsteps and nose breathing and there's Winslow Fromes, of all people, flanking me on my right. "What's going on?" he asks. He looks from Tyler to me then back at Tyler again. Then Tyler hands Winslow a plastic Safeway bag. There is something small and white—it looks like a tooth guard. Why would Tyler give a tooth guard to Winslow, who's wearing a T-shirt that says ACTUALLY I'M QUITE HUMBLE, WHICH IS RARE IN

PERSONS OF MY GENIUS AND CHARISMA. First Winslow and Petra then Winslow and Tyler. What's up in my upside-down world?

I am pretending to water ski with a wooden bathroom pass and I'm witnessing a very strange transaction.

Then Ms. Stuckley spins around. "What are the three of you standing there for?" She glares at Tyler. "I presume you have a teacher to annoy somewhere else in this building?"

Tyler gives a school-picture grin, waves, and shuffles away with his hands in his pockets. As I stand there in awe of his coolness, Ms. Stuckley snaps at me and Winslow. "Back to your seats immediately!"

"But I've got a bathroom pass!" I say. All eyes are on me as I bicycle-hold the pass. Ms. Stuckley clicks her tongue against her teeth. "Ernestine, did I say you could have the bathroom pass?"

"No, but . . . I . . ." Is she going to make me beg?

Ms. Stuckley sucks her teeth. She does this periodically to clean them. I guess she doesn't believe in dental floss. Yes, she is going to make me beg.

I get down on my knees. I am Ernestine. I have nothing to lose.

X Marks the Spot

"Historically, *x* is the favorite letter of a variable," Olivia says, absently drawing in her journal. "Also, *y* and *z* are popular members of the algebraic alphabet, too. *A*, *b*, and *c* represent a constant."

And that gets me thinking. If I were an algebraic expression, which part of me is *x*, representing change, and which part of me remains constant? Am I now more *x* than *a*?

ONE More to Go!

I look at his hand as Winslow scans each algebra problem during the break after orchestra. His hands are big, pretty much man-size, except without hair. He's aware of my staring, and I feel exposed. He doesn't look up at me, though. He goes back to his book, fascinated by something. Not by me. I guess.

I've got to get his attention. I remember the silly, playful Winslow in the library and I want him back. As Ernestine, it's MUCH harder to access that part of him. "Winslow, want to know how to find your celebrity name?" I ask impulsively.

"My what?" he asks, fiddling with the IN DOG YEARS I'M DEAD button on his canvas backpack.

"You heard me."

What's in a Name?

He leans closer to me and I can smell something musky. Deodorant? Aftershave? Yup, Winslow definitely shaved his chin because his little love patch has vanished. "Some people claim I've got extrasensory abilities," he says in a pseudo deep voice.

The first thing that pops into my head is that he's got X-ray vision and can see right through my clothes. I place my forearm in front of my chest and ask, "Can you read my mind?"

He taps his forehead. "Let's see. Something about . . ." He stands up. "You're thinking about the, um . . . let me see." He scratches his head. "The celebrity name game."

"YES!" I yell. "You're a bona fide, genuine, state-certified mind reader. Let's take the act on the road!" I grab his hand and raise it into the air, champion-style. His fingers feel solid, and surprisingly un-slimy. I'd almost like to hold his hand longer but, suddenly, I can feel my hand—can it be? Yes, a little sweaty. Holding Winslow's freaking hand is making me nervous. I find myself chewing extra hard on my piece of spearmint gum.

He gazes into my eyes and I swear the room is spinning a little. "I'm in," he says.

"In on what?" I say.

"You're such a flake. In on the name thing." He sighs. "I want to know *my* name."

"Your name? Winslow, you mean?"

"As in my other name. Stage name. Celebrity name."

"OHHHH. That name." Why do I feel shaky and so dumb? Calm thyself, *da*? *Calm thyself, da??* Why am I thinking in old English and Russian? Olivia's fault, no doubt. "Okay, take your first pet and the street you were born on and put them together and you have your celebrity star name. Mine's Mittens Manley," I say.

"That does sound like a celebrity name. A very frisky one. I'm Fluffy Harrington," he says. "More like a name for a big blond comedian." Then he leans toward me with this serious look on his face. "Can you take the gum out of your mouth? It's making me hungry."

"No. It's a fresh piece," I say.

"Got anything on you, food wise?"

I shake my head. "I think I'm starting to see a little drool."

"Right here?" he asks, tapping the left corner of his lip.

"No. Lower."

He points to his chin.

"No, higher," I say. "Maybe we should tape up your mouth."

"Duct tape. It's the answer for everything."

Lean and Green

In science, I stare at Tyler's head of hair. When I'm back to myself and we're dancing at Winterfest, I will get to see his awesome hair up close. It's so bright that I think it might glow in the dark.

He turns around for a moment, to pick up a pen, and then I get a look at his teeth, which are just as bright as his hair but without the greenish glow. But before he can pick up his pen, Justin does it for him. Tyler's like that. People just want to do things for him. The truth is I've never really heard Tyler talk that much. When he does, he seems cool. I'm sure whatever is inside will just come pouring out when we're together.

The only bad thing about me staring is that Olivia notices. Maybe because she's been scoping Tyler too. She gestures over at the back of his head. "Soooooo?"

"Yeeeeeeees?"

"I saw you looking," she says, not suppressing a smile. "Would thou like a spell to make someone all lovey-dovey?" She flicks her eyes at Tyler.

"*Me* looking? What about *you* looking?"

She shrugs. "He's a bit hard to miss. But Winslow's more my type. Since third grade I've known we're going to end up together." Olivia waves her arms so that they look rubbery. "See, I've been practicing on Winslow." She raises her eyebrows. "Fiddle-dee, I'm thinking that, yes, I will be going to the Winterfest Dance because I'm feeling increasingly confident that Winslow will show up and maybe dance with me. He acknowledged my presence three times today."

"Cool," I say, not knowing what to say because once again I'm starting to feel really bad. I'm trying to get Winslow to dance with me, too. Olivia is nicer than I thought. "About the spell. I'm okay for now, Olivia." Another lie that I must tell. Another way I suck.

When my science teacher tells me to get to work on writing up my lab, I just mumble, "Sure thing." Still can't remember his name. But I can tell you that he likes to wear big ugly silver rings with faces of tigers on them. Jewelry wise my mother and Mr. whatever-his-name-is would get along.

Now Presenting

Stuckley's oral report is due in five days and I'm in full-court press.

For the visual part of my oral presentation, I've used my mother's camera to photograph dogs. Can you believe it? Me with a complicated camera with lots of gizmos and gadgets? I actually asked her to show me how it works and to let me play around on Photoshop. And you know what? It wasn't horrible. Okay, it was kinda fun. The photos are to back up what I'm saying about the theme of *Oliver Twist*—that it's all about perception. I took a photo of this adorable corgi at the pound. I wish I could adopt him, but we aren't allowed to keep a dog at the stupid Sierra Garden Apartments. Another reason to loathe the place. And then I photographed a corgi dressed up in sweaters in front of a Spanish revival mansion in Atherton. I think it backs up my theme pretty well—similar dogs in different circumstances will be perceived differently.

A Big Fat Noob

On the board in social studies, I read something about Southern states wanting to retain their power, and the larger states wanting to have their power determined by popularity. No, population.

Oh, it's all the same.

All during social studies, I watch Winslow blink, lick his lips, and glance down at his notebook. Today, he's wearing a T-shirt with I KNOW I'M PSYCHIC 'CAUSE MY T-SHIRT SAYS MEDIUM. For some reason, Mr. Dribble actually makes him show his slogan to the class because he thinks it's *so* hysterical. I guess he's trying to show us that he has a sense of humor even while scaring us about the BIG TEST on Monday. But I'm not thinking test. I'm thinking Winslow.

His shoulders are broad. I hadn't noticed that before. And he's got a nice jawline, really solid. And . . . okay, wait.

Ew.

Out for the Count

Mr. Takashama taps his stick on his music stand. "Okeydokey. We don't have much time today, people. Concert's in four days, and if I catch anyone who's not ready I'll"—turning around, he reveals a pair of vampire teeth—"suck the blood, I mean music, right out of you."

The orchestra members roar appreciatively.

I notice Mr. Takashama wears big, dark black glasses as if he just stepped right out of a Buddy

Holly movie from the 1950s. His shiny black hair is floppy and looks very stylized. I'm almost jealous of its sheen. He turns toward me. "Ernestine, even if you're not able to join us, I hope you can share with your fellow players how to play the Bach concerto," he says, grinning. "Apparently, the members of our orchestra are unfamiliar with allegro."

Allegro? What language is he speaking? Portuguese? Spanish?

A thought jets into my mind. "Allegro" means "brisk and lovely." Oh, right. Ernestine's brain at work. Okay, it's one thing if part of me, the Ernestine part, understands what allegro is, but would my body actually know how to play the violin? That's not something I am willing to find out! Humiliation. Been there, done that.

This Thought Makes It Hard to Think About Studying for the Social Studies Test

For the first time, the silence of being alone in my house without cable TV or a DVR—Dad in L.A., Mom in one of her classes—doesn't bother me. My brain feels like a noisy, crowded house, as I read about that hot, sticky summer in August when a bunch of irritated guys yelled at one another in Philadelphia.

After spending all of Friday night studying about James Madison, Edmund Randolph, and the compromises and battles that eventually gave us the Constitution of the United States of America, I pull myself out of bed and onto the sticky floor. Welcome to my weekend! I studied so much I didn't think of Winslow. Okay, I'm thinking of Winslow now. But I can easily go back to the Colonial ponytailed dudes, right?

Hey, wait a minute, Winslow has a ponytail. But he's not a Founding Father.

Ahhhh!

A Winning Attitude

A glass of ancient apple juice and an opened, half-eaten apricot Fruit Roll-Up litter the floor. "This is disgusting!" Standing up, I kick the wall, stubbing my big toe.

I look at the aqua light on my digital alarm clock. It's already ten p.m. Soon enough it will be tomorrow. Monday. My social studies test.

I know Mom's back, watching television and folding clothes. She can't stand to do chores unless she's doing something entertaining at the same time.

I pad out into the living room, where Mom is

sprawled out on the couch watching a late-night Hallmark Hall of Fame weeper kind of thing. She's got a bowl of sesame sticks on the coffee table, an open bag of Pirate's Booty, and two glasses of natural soda. Unfolded T-shirts, giant panties and bras, and towels cover the floor.

Plopping down on the couch, I pick up a towel and fold it. "Mom, I did it. I'm *really* prepared for the test."

Mom's eyes are glued onto the TV, where a woman pleads with a state trooper to put out an APB on her missing child. She absently stuffs her mouth with Pirate's Booty.

"I'm going to get an A tomorrow," I say. "I can feel it. On a test." All by myself, I think.

"That's great, honey."

"I mean, I'm really, really ready."

My mom's glazed look mirrors her inactiveness. I want to cancel out her inactivity with my activeness. I want to shake her, shake the TV and throw it, and I want her to celebrate this moment because I am feeling prepared academically in a whole new way. Right now I'm feeling wired like I can't sleep, so I call Ninai and Olivia to ask if they are up for some late-night biking. Predictably, they both say no, so I go out for a ride by myself and the wind hitting my face feels good.

Later, when I gather the clothes to fold in my room, Mom says good night without a thank-you. But I don't need one. In the darkness, with only moonlight streaming through my window, I fold the towels and my underwear into neat little piles, using my hands as irons, pressing them into neat, organized bundles and color-coordinating them. Pinks in one pile. Yellows in another. My mom's nightgowns, towels. I find all of the matches for socks. And in the moonlight, I gaze at the neat stacks of laundry on the rug and feel satisfied.

Ready!

The bell is about to ring to signal the start of first period. The sky looks like Elmer's glue and the cold penetrates my bones. I'm almost glad to get to social studies.

As I move down the outdoor hallway, I pause in front of the water fountain. Pressing down on the button, I take a sip and a tinny taste washes over my tongue.

I shouldn't take another sip. Water, threatening to overflow, pools up inside the well. But my lips are so salty from the tofu omelet I ate at breakfast that I lean over to take one more drink. A tsunami splashes onto me—water, bits of toilet paper, and gum hit my cotton pants.

Naturally, at that moment, Caylin struts down the hallway, as the water drips down my nose. And there's Tyler, too, his hands in his front pockets, looking as cool as ever, while I am looking bad as ever, like I might as well have on my pajamas and fuzzy pink princess slippers. Tyler keeps on strutting down the hall. I don't even register with him but The Girls are peering at me and smirking in their I-have-a-secret way. My ugliness makes them feel prettier. I remember that feeling. I am not going to let them see me getting upset. It doesn't matter. At least I am prepared for the dumb social studies test. My hands grip the colored index cards with my notes so tightly that they curl in my fist.

I overhear some of their convo. Something about "the best . . . Winterfest . . . leadership . . . Limos . . . so so so the best thing . . . so so so . . . shopping . . . expensive . . . I accidentally bumped into a sixth grader Friday and he peed in his pants. . . . Hummer . . . blah blah . . . Tahoe."

I slink away, thinking about the Madison plan,

and the slave compromise, and the Liberty Bell, and letting freedom ring.

Duct Tape is Silver

Like a star-crazed fan, I race up to Mr. Dribble's desk and wave at him frantically. "It's me. I want to tell you something. I've actually studied."

"Very in-er-resting," he says, dropping the *t*. Then he leans over his desk and says under his breath, "Sometimes people fail and they're stuck just as they are. But when others go through transitions, you can't get in their way, no siree Bob. You wouldn't believe who Principal Barnes used to be, or me. That's another story." He waves his hand. "Can't go into it. Okay, if you really want to know. I didn't try hard enough, missed some opportunities, and missed the deadline. Anyhoo, so now I'm a middle school social studies teacher just trying to do some good deeds."

"The deadline. There's a deadline?"

"Yuk. Yuk. Yuk, you're funny. There's ALWAYS a deadline, gal. You know that."

"So if I don't get Winslow to dance with me at Winterfest then I'm forever . . . I mean . . ."

"You've determined your own deadline." He

wriggles his mustache. "Don't look at me."

"But . . . but . . ."

"But nothing. As much as I'd like to chat, I've got a test to give out on this lovely sunny day. Tests. You're familiar with them, right?" He fans out the stack of papers sitting on his desk. "Later," he says, rubbing his spazzed-out mustache with one hand and waving good-bye to me with the other.

Later? As Dribble turns his back and counts tests, Petra smiles at Winslow and sticks out her chest, while sucking in her breath. She's standing in the back of the classroom vogueing for—Winslow? Why is she doing that? She can't tolerate the idea of anything about him—his weird T-shirts—today a black one with a skull that says SILENCE IS GOLDEN. DUCT TAPE IS SILVER.

Petra taps his shoulder and says, all palsy-walsy, "Hey, Wins, help me with Dribble's dumb test. Will you, hon? With leadership, chairing the dance, volleyball, et cetera, I haven't had one second. Seriously. And I so appreciate all of the algebra homework, so if you'd help me out. Just this once. It'd be, like, such a HUGE favor."

I'm gasping with recognition. I know those words. That was me. All of the homework was for Petra!

The homework *I* had been doing for Winslow was because the boy was crushing hard on Petra Santora. That's why I've seen them chatting and whispering. *Hello.* It's all making sense now. Except for why he asked me to do the homework. I mean, he could have done it himself. I'm such an idiot.

Winslow shifts around on one foot. He's drooling at Petra, and I can tell that he thinks she's just more beautiful than an elf queen. She's taller than me but more filled out and has lashes that look fake because of all the mascara she globs there and is all shiny-lipped because of constant lip-gloss application. And her highlighted hair is never out of place because Petra is skilled with product. And she's strong-looking. Like a female kickboxer who could rip your head off and then kiss you hard.

Winslow springs out of his chair, hands Petra his study notes for the test, and puffs. "Have it. It's yours. I've got a copy on my computer." He clears his throat and raises his eyebrows. "Good talking online last night, *oui, ma cherie?* By the way, I found more top elf pickup lines. Ready?"

No! Could anyone *ever* be ready for top elf pickup lines?

Petra nods eagerly. *Huh?*

Winslow rubs his hands together and gets on his knees, I suppose in his best imitation of an elf. He looks up at Petra all googly-eyed. "Has anyone ever told you you have beautiful knees?"

Petra giggles.

"I can get you off the naughty list."

Another giggle. NO!

"I've got the keys to the sleigh tonight."

A burst of laughter.

"I'm a magical being. Put on your bikini for me."

Petra tugs on her shirt like she's going to lift it up. As if she actually has a bikini underneath her sweater. Puhlease. Talking online. Flirting in algebra. He. She. Could it be? The boy wears a chain, a ponytail, weird T-shirts, duct-taped shoes. He obviously doesn't care what anyone thinks about him.

Winslow takes a step toward Petra. "You meant what you said about *le dance*?" he says, rubbing his hands on his jeans. "I thought it was just, you know, *le joke*."

Petra leans forward, tapping his chin with her finger. "Wins, if you'll help me out with the test, nothing's a joke."

"You'll do aneee-thing, won't you?" says Winslow.

Petra smiles at him big.

NOOOOOOOOO! How could a normal, sane,

adolescent boy be rendered powerless by his hormones when a certain kind of girl goes to work on him? It's sick. Sick and way too familiar.

I yank the sheet away. "Don't, Winslow!"

"You're such a freak," says Petra, squinting at me like I'm a blinding strobe light. She winks at Caylin and then cups her hand around her mouth and leans into Winslow. "Too late for study notes. I'm going to need some *personal* assistance."

The Arrangement

"It would really mean a lot to me, Wins." She glances at his T-shirt. "I love that on you. You're getting SO cute these days. Seriously. Right, Cay?"

Caylin's eyes graze over his face, resting on his Saturn eyes, which are definitely his best feature. "Totally."

I can feel my breath catching in my throat and want to scream. I'm also standing in the back of the classroom, far away from Dribble, whose back is still turned as he counts out his tests. But I'm paranoid that somehow he'll hear me, even though it's totally noisy and everyone is speaking at once. But still, I have to say something. My voice rises an octave as I glare at Petra and Caylin and whisper hoarsely, "You shouldn't lie to Winslow like that."

Caylin bites her bottom lip. "Not me. Honestly. I think Wins is getting cute. Don't get upset, Ernestine." She sucks in her breath. "Petra's in trouble. Big-time. She's already gotten one detention. One more thing and she's out of here. I'm serious. Her mom will pull her from La Cambia and lock her up in the Hillwood School." She emphasizes the last part because everyone knows the Hillwood School is a place where you have to grow your own granola and eat it for lunch.

"For real?" I ask. But I know that she's serious. Caylin's eyes give it away—they're already a little puffy and reddish. I remember when Petra told her that her thighs were jiggly on the same day that Ms. Stuckley had given her a C-plus on a paper and her father had married the witch. It was a very bleary, red-eyed day.

"I'd like to help you," says Winslow, studying Petra. "I mean *really* like to help you, *ma chérie*." He is one of the only eighth-grade guys who is actually Petra's height. "But my seat's a mile away from yours." He points to Petra's seat by the bank of windows, then his, which is near the front by the whiteboard. Dribble had moved him a couple of days ago so he could make sure that Winslow was paying attention and not reading one of his half-human books. "See, not possible," he says in a bad French accent. "Unless we warp time and space, that is." Squinting his eyes, he taps his chin. "Falling into a black hole. With you. Could be interesting." He squints at her. "Nah, it'd ruin your hair."

Dribble suddenly stands up and clears his throat. "Please sit down in your seats, gals and guys. It's showtime. I mean, test time!"

Sliding his overloaded book bag down his broad hulking shoulders (Has he lost weight? Gotten taller?), Winslow gazes at me intently like he used to when I was Taffeta. "How about you, Ernestine? Are you in a helpful mood?"

Me? "What?" I feel like jumping on Winslow's head and making it one-dimensional. "That homework was for Petra."

He grins.

"I thought it was for you."

"Me?" He guffaws. "I take Algebra Two at Menlo Atherton. Why would it be for me?" That's right. Duh! Winslow leaves during gym to go the high school. How could I have forgotten?

"Why don't you do it yourself?" I hiss.

"Why would I when you were so willing?"

How could he do this to me? Do I have a choice?

I grit my teeth so that I don't throw my social studies book at him. Calm thoughts. Think about something soothing like clouds or Cherry Garcia ice cream. Don't blow it. Keep the course. Okay, I can now manage a pretend smile at the complete jerk. My lips are chapped, though, and I can feel them sticking to my teeth.

Petra gazes at me like I really exist. "So, it's a yes?"

Test Me!

"Just a few answers," I say.

Petra holds up her hand, crossing her fingers. "I swear, I won't bother you or any of your brainiac friends today." She smiles at me like I'm a member of the Special Olympics. I can remember playing Marco Polo in her pool, and sneaking in to my first PG-13 movie to watch with her when we were eleven. She made me laugh so hard once I actually peed in my pants in the movie theater. Okay. Okay. What's the big deal? Right? Karmically, after all of those times with Winslow, it's only right that I let someone cheat off of me for once. Dribble is whistling and all happy, and I think he'd appreciate my generosity.

"Okay, but don't copy my essay," I whisper jokingly to Petra, "because I'm writing about Dadaism and the duality of existence in the Constitutional Convention."

"Whatever, Ernie," she says, slapping me on the back. "You're a very nice brain."

Dribble carefully passes out the tests and lays them on our desks delicately like they're snowflakes about to melt. He clucks his tongue. "Alrighty, you've got fifty minutes, folks. We've spent a lot of weeks studying the Constitution of the good U.S. of A. If you know what's good for you, I'd suggest you show me that you've been paying attention." He glances up at the clock. "You may start now."

The fill-in-the-blank sections are easy. No surprises there, but Petra keeps on kicking me under the desk so I can spread my paper over to the right corner and she can lean over and copy. She has really good eyesight, and seems to be able to read my answers without even straining forward. A definite talent.

I can feel it in my gut. I've gotten everything—all of the answers—right. There isn't one that I don't know. Bubbles inside of bubbles. Patterns in patterns. I'm finding the function in dysfunction. Who would have thought it? Does that mean I am comfortable being dysfunctional or does it mean I am functioning back to my true self?

When I start the essay section, Petra kicks me hard in the shin. But I won't budge. No way will I do that for her.

I'm almost the last one to turn in my paper, and Petra's the first. When I hand Dribble my paper, he nods at me but doesn't say anything. My heart pounds in my ears and in my throat. To my left, I can't see Olivia's face because of her hair hanging down, but I can hear the scratching of her calligraphy pen on paper. Ninai writes more slowly and carefully. Her eyes catch mine and she smiles. Wow, Ninai actually does look good in that Girl Scout getup.

When the bell rings and I'm finished, I tell myself that everything's going to be okay.

I stroll down the hall, imagining the A-plus written in red ink at the top of my paper. What would my mom say? Of course, Ernestine was used to doing well all of the time academically. But Taffeta wasn't. I grip my leg, pinching extra flesh that never used to be there. I squeeze hard. Is Tafettta even there at all?

Suddenly, Winslow

I mean, he's really close and, as he sort of slam-dances into me, we make contact at the hip. "Hey," he says.

"Hey," I say idiotically. He smells like pencil shavings and Cool Ranch tortilla chips.

Walking backward, Winslow starts singing some old Rolling Stones song that my mom likes. "Hey, hey, you, you, get off of my cloud." Is this code for *go away*? Because part of me wants to go away. Far away from Winslow. I backpedal a bit but he continues to sing, and steps right up to me so we're practically nose to nose. "See you at the dance," he singsongs. His chain clanks to the beat.

I'm so surprised, I drop my pencil. He's ACTUALLY going to be there. I remember that this is good news.

"You're going?" I ask.

"Yeah." He stuffs his hands into his pockets. "Surprised? I made a deal, right?"

"Me. Petra. Who else do you have going?"

"Ew, you sound *jalouse*." He tugs on the end of his ponytail.

"No. It's just that you've selected another untouchable girl."

"Another? What are you talking about?"

Can I say, *First Taffeta and then Petra*? No. That I'm detecting a pattern? No? "Stop nitpicking. I just mean Petra's not seriously gonna give you a second look."

"I've got plans," says Winslow.

"Plans?" I ask.

"Yes."

"Like?"

"Like you'll just have to see," says Winslow, smiling mysteriously. What could he possibly mean? What could Winslow Fromes possibly do to make himself more attractive to Petra?

"Great. I'm so happy for you, Winslow."

He raises his eyebrows. "You are?"

"Yeeeeees, of course."

He shifts his weight on his duct-taped shoes. "See you there?"

"Yeah," I say calmly so I don't seem desperate. I expected to be all tingly, screaming WAHOO at full amplification but, instead, I feel almost blank. What's up with that?

I want to say *Petra has no intention of dancing with you*. I want to tell him SOOO badly because I can't stand how happy he is. But then he wouldn't show up to the dance and Olivia would be bummed, and I'd be uber bummed. Because I'd be stuck as the un-me for the rest of my life.

I miss Taffeta!

Doing a Happy Dance

Before English, Olivia strolls up to me, tucking her hair around her ears so that for the first time I see she has eyes. "How did you do on the test, my dear little Ernestineski?"

"I did all right." My throat constricts. It's small now, so small that I'm sure a grain of rice can't fit down it. I'm sure I'll need Ensure, the pink vitamin stuff my grandfather had to drink. That's how I feel when I think about cheating for Petra. I need life support.

"All right?" She laughs and bends down to double-knot my shoelaces together. "I won't unknot them until you tell me the truth."

"Okay, whatever," I say, flagging my hand. "I did *really* well."

She hugs me. "Piffies, bonkies, and sassafras tea! I'm so happy for you." Then Olivia smiles mysteriously, like she's Mona Lisa with crooked teeth. "And I did something very well too. I have the most wonderful information," says Olivia, who starts to hum for a moment. "I heard Winslow is definitely going to Winterfest this year. It's because I've unleashed my woo-woo powers." She waves her hands witchily. "We're going to dance all night, which means you and Ninai must—and I'm not accepting any nos—must ignore reason and sanity and accompany me to Winterfest. Okay? Don't say you won't. Don't *even* think it."

I sit there for a moment, moving my lips but no words are coming out. Then I manage to say, "Wow." For a moment, I really want to tell Olivia EVERYTHING! That Winslow will be there because of Petra, that I'm already planning to go to Winterfest and dance with Winslow. But I can't snatch her moment. I've been a thief all my life.

I begin to cry. "Yes, I'll go to Winterfest. Omigod. It's what you always . . . wanted, Olivia. It's like the universe is calling out to you and saying, *Go for it!* That's wonderful," I say, choking out the words.

Olivia's eyes water. "You are *such* a good friend. I'm *so* lucky."

I know I am happy for Olivia but I am crying for me. It feels so good to release. I continue to babble how proud I am of her as the warm tears streak down my big fat cheeks. My tongue tastes the saltiness. I feel like I'm letting the inside out. Not in control anymore. I'm being real. For once in my life, I'm being real.

Liar, Liar on the Telephone Wire

"Dad," I gush into the phone. "My oral report in English. I have it *so* nailed. I'm, like, actually looking forward to tomorrow. And you know that guy I was telling you about? The one I might be, you know, hooking up at the dance with? Well, he said he's going but—"

"Ah, man, Ernestine. I knew he would. Otherwise, he'd be a total and complete idiot and I'd have to fly up and wail on the dude."

"Dad," I groan into the receiver, about to explain everything but then I decide against it. I don't tell him that he's not going because of me but because of Petra and that I'm about to ruin my friendship with Olivia. And that I'm not myself. It's waaaaaay too complicated.

He pauses. "So is it formal or informal?"

"Informal, Dad. But lots of girls, you know, find something kind of special for the day."

"I see," he says.

"I'm sure I'll figure something out."

"I'm sure," he says. "I know it. All good stuff. How's your mom?" I'm surprised. He doesn't normally ask about her.

"Busy. You know, with her photography and wearing pajamas twenty-four–seven."

"Well, good for her. Keeping busy. I've had some good conversations lately with some big fish about the screenplay." I start to space out as he goes on about big agencies versus hands-on managers. Normally, I'm really good at listening to everything my dad has to say about Hollywood stuff, but my mind wanders and I make sure to say, "Uh-huh" at the appropriate places.

Winslow will be at Winterfest. All I have to do now is get him to dance with me.

The Day After

Dribble stands in front of the class waving a stack of tests like a flag. "Anyhoo, I was very pleased, folks. But there were some of you I was NOT happy with at all." Dribble never loses it and yells. He waggles his mustache and licks his dry, pale lips.

I wait to be that very pleasing person.

Dribble hands back the tests row by row and I see that Caylin has an A-minus. I did better. I know that. And Winslow gets an A. Big surprise. Tyler drums on his desk like he's pleased with his C-plus.

And I close my eyes as the paper drops onto my desk with a soft whosh. When I open them I see a big F and a "See me after class." As Petra gets her paper, I hear her go, "Oh, man. He caught us."

Us, I thought. *How about* you, *honey bunny?*

As Dribble goes through the test I can hardly breathe. I'd gotten every answer correct. Every single stupid one, but *still* he'd given me an F. So not fair. I didn't do the cheating. I'd been cheaten upon. What's up with that?

Killer Choice

When the bell chimes for the end of first period, I zip up to Dribble's desk. "I got all the answers right."

"Yes, you did," says Dribble, "and so did *she*." He nods over at Petra who stands at the opposite side of the desk. She's looking down at her mauve-covered nails.

"But I wasn't the one who cheated," I blurt.

"I'm sorry, Ernestine." Cocking his mostly bald head side to side, he cups his ear. "But I heard you agree to let Petra there have a look-see." He heard that? *Freak.* He eyes Petra. "Did you or did you not ask Ernestine if you could look at her work?" Patting the ends of his flyaway comb-over, he grimaces. "Ma'am. A simple question. Yes or no?"

Petra puckers her nose. "No."

"No?" Dribble stares her down. His squirrely mustache quivers. "NO?"

Slamming down her notebook onto the desk, Petra yells, "YES! OKAY. Okay." I'm not used to seeing Petra so easily defeated but it figures she would be mad about it. She uses her temper as a way to control people.

Even though my throat feels as blocked up as a La Cambia water fountain, I give a Taffeta smile, sliding my lips back over my teeth, and then remember I'm not that girl anymore. I don't need to look happy.

Dribble knocks his forehead with his fist as if he thought of something. "This incident means consequences, such as the NP, as in No Privileges, list."

The FREAKIN' NP list. "This isn't fair," I say. "You're punishing me for letting Petra cheat off me but you didn't punish Winslow when he let me cheat off of him."

Petra stares at me, completely confused. "You, of all people, cheated?"

I wave my hand in front of me. "It's hard to explain."

"Exactly, it's hard to explain. Anyhoo. I'm the teacher and you're the student. And I have my teacherly reasons for everything." Scratching his chin, he peers at me. "If you prefer you can have a fresh start." I can't do this. There is NO WAY I'LL EVER take any more of Dribble's so-called help. But I can't go NP, either, for obvious reasons. Like I won't have the right to go to Winterfest.

Petra, suddenly, loses the sour look in her face. "Whatever it takes. Give me a fresh start. I'm so there."

No, Petra. Please. Don't do it. But my lips don't move. No words. She'll think I'm insane, a mess, and she'd be right.

Dribble stares at me, drumming his fingers on his desk.

I swallow, but the knot in my throat doesn't unravel. It's a killer choice—if I take a fresh start, who will I become next? But if I get punished and on NP, it's a lose-lose.

No! Principal!

Mom and I sit in scratchy green chairs, facing Mrs. Barnes and her frowny face. I'm not used to that. Normally, she's all teeth and dimples. In fact, behind her desk are no less than three photographs of Caylin and her sister Phoebe all gummy-smiling. One from Squaw Valley, sitting on a ski lift, and a couple of soccer team photos, too. I know it's crazy, but I feel like they're mocking me.

Mrs. Barnes straightens the papers on her desk that looked perfectly in place already. "I was very disappointed in you, Ernestine." Then she sighs heavily and sits back against her chair. *And I've been very disappointed in you, Mrs. Barnes. You're planning on cheating this whole school, Mrs. Barnes, with your little testing plan. Wait until all of the ESL students are down visiting their families in Mexico and then test us so you can keep up appearances.* I want to scream at her, but instead I'm listening to her go, "You're now on No Privileges, which as I'm sure you know means no field trips or school dances." Oh, God. Why did I choose NP?

I want to good-girl nod politely, but this "NO!" bursts from my lips.

Mom squeezes me on the shoulder. "It doesn't seem so bad."

Further blurtation: "YOU CAN'T DO THIS!"

For a moment, Mrs. Barnes closes her eyes like she can't bear the sight of such an out-of-control child. She purses her lips at Mom, like I'm her fault. But Mom, as always, is oblivious. She smoothes her wild hair. "It will give you time to think about your actions. And it's not like you were dying to go to school dances anyway."

Whatever

Idiot Winterfest posters cover every imaginable wall, even in Dribble's class.

Experience Moonlight Magic
at Winterfest
Friday, December 19
Dance the nite away
in The Gym!
$3.00 at the door
6:30-9:00 p.m.
Pictures with Santa or Snow Scene-$1.00
Brownies = $ .50
Chips= $1.00
Drinks = $ .75
Sponsored by 8th-Grade Leadership

If I could rip off every poster in this school, I would.

I glare at the smiling little girl in a Santa hat riding a reindeer. It looks like a first-grade Christmas party. I'd LOVE to be able to tell Mr. Dribble about how this isn't working out one little bit! I'd like to tell him how stupid his class is, his ugly mustache, his freaky self. But who cares? It doesn't matter now. I stare at the poster of the dance, and then I claw it off the wall.

No Dance. No Life.

"Here," I say, handing Ms. Stuckley the notecards and photographs for my presentation.

"It's an oral report, Ernestine," says Ms. Stuckley, tapping her nose ring. The point is how you verbally execute your presentation."

I swallow for a moment. Ms. Stuckley stares at me. "It's been a really, really bad day," I say. Then I start to cry a little.

She pulls up her grade book and I wait for her pseudo British lips to go, "F!" Instead she says, "Make it up when you're feeling better. Tomorrow, I hope."

"Thank you. Thank you *so much*."

"You always turn everything in on time, even early. So this one time, I can offer you a little reprieve." She writes an incomplete next to my name. Incomplete, that's me.

Busted!

I want to bolt out the door to the music room, but Beatle wannabe and orchestra cheerleader Mr. Takashama says, "I'm not letting your modesty get the better of you this time. I called your mother and she says that you don't have nor have ever had tendonitis." As the bell to end fifth period rang five minutes ago, all of the other string players rush past me. They have put away their instruments and are psyched to hang with their friends during break.

I'm psyched to get out of this room. This life.

I am such a lame-o. I can't even speak. Instead, I sit down on a chair looking at a sea of notes on a music stand. I have no idea what any of the squiggles mean. I know they're notes of some kind, but after that I'm lost.

"It's okay, Ernestine," says Mr. Takashama. "It's called performance anxiety. I used to get it too, when I was your age. But I don't like the fact that you had to hide this from me and invent lies. You could have simply told me the truth and I would have understood. You nailed that Bach concerto weeks ago, but you still wanted more. I get it. But I'm telling you it's okay. Whatever you do tonight when you play at the concert will be okay."

"I'm going to play?'

He nods. "I think it would be the best thing you can do for yourself to get over this hump."

My stomach slouches. Beads of sweat pour down my forehead. Everything is swirling. How am I going to do this?

Science

Today, of all days, I remember my science teacher's name. Maybe it's because I'm staring at a poster in our room announcing that testing is going to take place in January this year instead of April. Maybe it makes me so mad what Mrs. Barnes is planning on doing to the ESL students that it jogs memory cells. Even though I know who he, my science teacher, is, I still don't like dissecting a cow's eyeball. I think vegetarians should have alternatives, like maybe dissecting a daisy or something. I'll have to talk to Ninai about this and get her to help me start a campaign. Oh, here's the weird part. My science teacher's name is Mr. Butcher, so bizarrely appropriate.

The Winter Concert

I am swinging my violin madly now and Ninai is staring at me. "It's supposed to be good for the wood. Good air flow." Now my violin is going to accidentally but conveniently bash against the stand and splinter apart. Oh, well. I grab it by the handle with little wooden peg thingies and aim for direct impact, when Mr. Takashama yanks the violin out of my grasp.

"I don't think your mother would appreciate having to pay for a new violin." Mr. Takashama crouches in front of me, cradling the violin as if it's a baby. "You better be okay. I'm not taking no for an answer because the concert is starting in"—he looks at his watch—"five minutes."

I think it's time for me to bolt. Maybe I'll go to Antarctica. I don't think they have violins down there.

Somehow

There isn't one empty seat. Parents stand in the aisles. Grandparents hold programs (expertly calligraphed by Olivia) and snap photos. And my mother is MIA. She said she'd be there but would be running from a class in Palo Alto. I didn't protest when she warned me that she'd be late. It's not like I actually want her to see me sucking in front of hundreds of people. But somehow I'm here, sitting in this folding chair, my violin tuned and on my lap.

Somehow, I couldn't bail on orchestra because, maybe, I'm just a little bit curious about what will happen if I actually try to play. Or maybe it's that I want to punish myself.

Mr. Takashama is wearing a hat with a menorah on top. His wife, who's Jewish, made it for him.

It's my Bach solo. Waving his baton into the air, he motions to me so I pick up my violin.

Out of the corner of my eye, I see a woman burst into the back of the auditorium with a floppy hat. Mom! Late but here. I pick up the violin and put it under my chin. I can feel all the eyes. The stage lights laser onto my back. A trickle of sweat tickles my shoulder blades. I can hear all of the collective breathing of the crowd. Mr. Takashama waves his baton into the air and he nods at me.

And I begin to play.

Somehow my arm remembers notes. My wrist knows how to bow, my arms know the proper way to stroke back and forth across the four strings. Am I reading the notes? I stop thinking, stop caring, and give in to the music. Why didn't I trust myself earlier? My mind knew. It knew algebra. It knew Dadaism. Why not violin? I feel my body swaying. Some notes make me angry, others so crazy sad it clouds my chest with sadness. *How am I doing this? How did I never do this before?*

After I'm done, Mr. Takashama plunks back in his Dracula teeth. Everyone's clapping. My orchestra teacher smiles, fangs and all. They're clapping for me, even Winslow.

My mom takes photos. I can feel her flash because it's so bright. Despite the urge, I do not duck.

Congrats!

Afterward, all of the kids I've ever avoided my whole life rush at me to congratulate me on my solo, but my mom gets to me first. Her arms circle me into a hug. "That was SO amazing," she says. "You didn't miss a note and you remembered not to rush. There was SO much feeling. I am so proud, Little Love."

The words penetrate and I feel like crying because I might be stuck like this forever and all of this encouragement is making me feel guilty for wanting Taffeta back. Out of the corner of my eye, I see Winslow shuffle up to Sneed and help him put away his cello and he gives me a thumbs-up and I want to kill him. How dare he remind me of my stuck here-ness.

"That was SO good," says Ninai, patting my arm.

I hear the jangle of Olivia's bracelets on her arm and she's smiling with her crooked teeth, her hennaed hair flowing in front of her face. "Magical," she breathes.

As I put my violin away, I spot Justin picking up trash around the perimeter of the auditorium. He launches a Coke can into the garbage. "What is he doing that for and why did he come to an orchestra concert?" I ask Ninai, who's navigating her cello around a bunch of stands.

"He's officially on NP for egging a bunch of

teachers' cars. But Mrs. Barnes is allowing him to do something positive so he can go to the dance."

"Something positive?" My heart goes staccato and then it's drumming allegro fast. Something positive. I can do that.

The Next Day in Mrs. Barnes's Office

"But you let Justin get off NP by doing something positive," I say.

Mrs. Barnes fingers her blue pin ID which reads PRINCIPAL. "But Justin asked."

"Okay, so now I'll ask." I stare at her pleadingly. I smile and look remorseful. "How can I do something positive? Just tell me and I'm there."

Pressing her palms together, Mrs. Barnes leans forward across the desk. "What could you do? I'll give you a clue." She sits up straight in her chair. "Something meaningful. That's what you can do."

"Sweep? Paint?"

"Ernestine, this is not a guessing game. Give it some time and when you have a real answer, get back to me."

"But I don't have time. I have to go to Winterfest tomorrow. Not being able to go to the dance *is* a HUGE punishment," I say.

"It's a taking away of rewards," she explains like she's memorized a textbook. "Not punishment. A punishment would be if I made you do fifty push-ups right now." She turns up her lips into a tight smile. "Believe me, I'd actually prefer that you do something positive."

"Then let me go to the dance tomorrow." And then I think to myself, *If you wanted to do something positive, don't worry so much about your precious scores. Don't cheat. Worry about your students needs.* All *of your students.*

Mrs. Barnes cups her chin. Is she actually considering letting me go? "I can't let you go to the dance 'officially,'" she says, making quotations in the air. "But I do have an idea. How about if you go to the dance as a leadership helper?"

A helper to Petra and Caylin. She doesn't mean "helper." She means "slave"!

Invisible to Invisibles

LEADERSHIP still needs more Santa 's Little Helpers for the Winterfest Dance on December 19. Sign-up during lunch today in the gym. That 's right! Hang with your bffs and make decorations in the gym for Winterfest today and find out how you can help make Winterfest the best dance ever! See u there. Just two more days! It 's gonna be a PARTY!

I stare at the sign posted outside the gym. Actually, the new gym. Our school has two. This is the state-of-the art, funded-by-bond-money one, since, as Mom likes to point out, people like to pay money for buildings and not teachers. The gym only a couple of weeks ago felt like home, but now my stomach lurches thinking about stepping into it. Everything smells so new, even the plantings. I pull on some ornamental grass and snap off a twig from one of the trees, take a deep breath, and force my legs to plow forward. Then I reluctantly open the door and see Caylin holding court.

"Omigod," says Caylin to her crowd and gives her best gummy smile. "I'm, like, so overwhelmed. Seriously. You guys are the best. I mean it. We're going to have so much fun this year. It's going to be amazing." She claps her hands. Even Petra is looking at Caylin like the rah-rah stuff is going too far. "Anyway, to be"—she makes quotes in the air like her mom—"'officially' a Santa's Little Helper, you have to work the dance for one hour either as a refreshment server, snowflake photo assistant, or clean-up elf." Then, she pulls out a Santa's hat. "You get to wear this the day of the dance, and girls, guess what?—you get to keep it as a little thank-you for aaalllll your haaaaard work."

The two dozen girls lining up in front of the stage actually all jump up and down.

"So, who's in?" Caylin's overly enthusiastic, high-pitched voice rings through the crowd.

Every single hand in the gym goes up, including mine. As Caylin continues speaking about the fabulousness of what they're doing, Maggie the Mushroom goes around very importantly writing down everyone's name. Her invisible friend tails her every move with her oh-so-fabulous clipboard.

Then Petra, hand on hip, tosses her head, tinkling the bell on her Santa cap. Should I warn her about the Fresh Start that is heading her way? Make her believe me? If the tables were turned, I'd want her to do the same for me. I'd have to wait for an opportunity to say something but, the truth is, part of me would like to see her punished so she could understand what I'm going through.

"Listen up, girls," goes Petra in her most booming, bossy voice. "This afternoon, we're going to make decorations. Isn't that the best? You're about to be my heroes." She points to the different stations and, before I know it, everyone's either painting red stockings above a cardboard fireplace, or cutting out a sleigh, or taping giant yellow and pink snowflakes to black paper, which covers the walls of the gym. I feel like a freak standing ALONE while everyone else is chatting madly away with someone, glitter glue pen in hand, making ugly, two-dimensional decorations.

New Strategy: Look for someone who's standing off by themselves.

Like Maggie the Mushroom's Invisible Friend

I sashay toward her, and then think, *If she only knew who was approaching her, she'd angst.* In all the time I've known her at La Cambia, I don't think I've EVER been the first one to start a convo. In fact, I don't think I've ever talked to her at all.

Well, here's your big chance, Invisible Girl. "Hey," I say, all friendly and enthusiastic-like. "I'm Ernestine."

She turns around, pushing her drab brown hair out of her drab pale face. "I'm Meshell. Spelled like 'me' and then the word 'shell,' like the beach."

"Oh," I say, nodding like this is fascinating information. It's strange, but all of the times that she sat with Maggie Milner I had NO idea that she had a name. I mean, I knew she had a name but I could never remember it. Meshell is a little bit chunky. Her makeup is heavy. As Caylin passes by, she gives Meshell a smile but does not catch my eye.

Time to begin small talk. "It's freezing in this gym," I say, jumping up and down.

"Uh-huh," says Meshell-like-the-beach.

"Glad I remembered my jacket."

"Know what you mean." But her brown eyes are glazing over. She's looking beyond me for someone more "interesting" to speak with right now. Standing up on her heels, she peers at Caylin, who's demonstrating the technique for putting the maximum amount of glitter on decorations. And now, it seems, *I'm* the invisible one.

Believe Me

Sitting on a folding chair, Petra is bent over signing someone's cast with Wite-Out. And I get this other snapshot of her, when I had broken my collarbone. She and Caylin came over with a new iPod fully loaded with all of my favorite songs and a box of Trader Joe's organic truffles. She can be so motherly at times.

Then a Guy strolls into the gym. Sure, there are already a few boys helping out, the nice, forgettable types who are polite and somewhat athletic and are neither geeky nor cool but get their Brownie points by putting up posters for Leadership girls and lifting boxes. But *this* Guy is different. Big for eighth grade with yellowish eyes that are fringed with dark lashes. Square jaw. A preppy white polo and baggy khakis. Then I notice he lumbers in this familiar way. A sort of shuffle of someone who is heavy or flat-footed. It's . . . I'm blinking now. It's . . .

"Winslow?"

"He's hot," I heard a voice say.

"Where's the black T-shirts with the weird sayings? And that chain?"

"Where's the ponytail? And the duct-taped shoes?"

Lots of whispers. And my world is, once again, folding into itself. He's not glancing at me at all. I mean, I see his eyes literally sweep past me as if I'm standing in a black hole in another dimension. His eyes are locking with Petra and he is even checking out Mushroom Girl for a second. Suddenly, I picture a convo I would have with him as Taffeta. I'd stand right in front of him and just say, "Hey." Just one word. No touching required and he'd register this look of shock and awe because he'd be blown away with gratitude.

Winslow grabs a stack of red-and-green posters for Winterfest, and leaves the way he came, back out the double doors. He's volunteering, helping out with Leadership?

He cut off his ponytail.

He's wearing a polo and white canvas rubber-soled shoes, like he's a prep or something, like he actually cares about looking like he walked out of a catalog for boys who sail.

Why? Now I don't care about being subtle. My world *has* to stop changing.

NO!

I'm going to stop my world from changing NOW!

"PETRA!" I scream, picking up a megaphone. "I've got something to say to you!"

The Girls stop their stapling and taping and whispering. They whirl around to face me. "It's not worth getting out of it, Petra. Something REALLY bad will happen to you."

"Something really bad will happen?" asks Caylin, squinting. "That's not good."

"Yeah, I'll have to look at this loser's face," says Petra.

Loser, ouch. That really hurts. I remember in sixth grade Petra wanted to start a winner's club. Just me, Caylin, and her. Each of us was a winner, she said.

Me in swimming. I have three Far Western winning times in freestyle and backstroke, and Caylin's won tons of singing competitions, and Petra's a volleyball diva. So she bought each of us a little bracelet with a trophy charm. She said to touch that trophy when you were feeling down, like maybe today things wouldn't go your way and you'd be a loser. Without thinking, I went to brush my wrist with my finger to feel for my bracelet. But the trophy charm was not there. Guess it never was now.

News alert: I seem to be stuck in loser mode.

Then EXTREME blurtation: "Look at me, Petra. Just look at me! Do you think I was always like this? I used to be just like you. My name used to be Taffeta Smith and I cheated and Dribble turned me into this. Ernestine. It's not me. You, Petra, used to be my best best friend and Caylin, too. But I kind of ruled. So I hope you're planning on really dancing with Winslow like you promised because if you don't you will really REALLY hurt his feelings."

Caylin backs away. "You're really scaring me." But then she gazes at me for a moment, a probing look as if she sees something she recognizes. I want to fling my arms around her but then I realize there's something on my face. I brush my cheek and a little silver moon decoration flutters to the floor.

MIA

"Catch." Ninai tosses me a paperback and I see that it has an actual freakin' unicorn on the cover. *The Last Unicorn* by Theodore Sturgeon. "Short stories," says Ninai. "They're amazing, sort of mind-bending, twisted, full of horror and beautiful at the same time. You'll love it."

"Thanks," I say. "I could use a little escape." And that's not a lie. There's already been some backlash to my outburst with Petra.

My undies are MIA.

It happened after gym class. I went to check my locker and found my shirt hanging on the hook, my jeans, and flip-flops, but no pair of light blue panties. Heading back to class felt like riding a sandpaper saddle. I had a permanent wedgie. On the way back, I'd stop every five feet or so, which means I got a good look at all of the posters for the dance in the hallway. The dance is tomorrow. Why do I feel SICK?

TPed

After school, Mom's up, pacing back and forth in the

living room. "Yes, I'll hold," she snaps, then covers the receiver with her hand and says to me, "I can't believe this."

"Believe what?"

Mom waves her hand for me to be quiet and gets back on to the phone. "Yes, but it's not. No. No. Yes." As she steps over sesame sticks imbedded into the carpet, she whispers to me. "He's holding us responsible."

"Who?"

"Mr. Langley, our apartment manager. Jerk. It's because whenever he comes here to fix anything the place is a mess. He never makes an appointment. He just shows up. And then I have to make an excuse. I've been working late with some photo gigs and haven't been in the house but he's eyeing everything. The dishes in the sink." She starts to turn on the water and looks down. "Where's the sponge, Ernestine? Do you know where the sponge is?" She dashes around, looking for it on the kitchen table. The sofa. "I just need the sponge; then I could do the freaking dishes. That's all. Do you know where it is?"

I stroll over to the sink. "Try the little compartment here, Mom. The one that flips out above the cabinet."

"Thank you, honey. You're amazing. Incredible!"

She pulls away. "Did I tell you that? My daughter is amazing!" Then she starts to cry.

"What's going on, Mom? Spill."

"Look outside." She gestures toward the picture window that looks out over the parking lot.

I yank on the plastic shade, and at first, I don't see anything, just the red-shingled 1970s Mission-style apartment complex, but when I look again I see it. On the balcony, there's shaving cream all over the grill and the rusty lawn furniture. Toilet paper in the live oak and palm trees. In purple Silly String on a red truck in the parking lot, I can make out the words: I'M A SOLOIST! Also on the truck, the words:

Wash Ernestine 's hair
Freak
Makeup is a waste on your face!

A memory needles into my head. Last year, TP'ing Olivia's apartment in Lower Sharon Heights. Totally covering her father's old Honda and all of the trees in front with pink toilet paper. It was around the time we had e-mailed Olivia pretending to be Tyler. I shake the thought away.

This is really mean—and only a few girls are capable of this kind of thing. And the worst part? I used to be one of them. And then I wonder something. Why am I feeling like someone is using my chest as a trampoline? It's like each breath feels labored and my throat feels bent like a straw. I mean they are not even talking about me. I'm not really Ernestine. It's not my face or my hair they are REALLY commenting on. But somehow it is. Algebraically speaking, I'm a constant and not a variable. And this apartment, the one with the naked boy statue and the crumbly red-tile roof is my house where my mother and I live. My house, the big one in Menlo Park, was also my house. It was where my family lived. I thought it would go on that way forever, but it didn't. I had a life once there where I had two parents living together, and enough money that shopping was just another one of my extracurricular activities. And now I have a new life and the old one is disappearing like a dream. Am I Taffeta still, Ernestine still, or something in between?

Cleanup Crew

"What's wrong, Ernestineski?" Olivia asks. "What's going on? Tell me."

I press my lips together, prepared to be stoic, even on the phone.

"Did Petra and her worshippers do something?"

"Yes," I say, and she curses under her breath in something that sounds like a cross between Russian and Martian. Before I can help it, I'm crying into the cell and spewing all of the details.

"Ninai and I will be right over," says Olivia. "I just can't believe them. I would love to turn those brats into little pink naked mole rats. Would you like that?"

This discussion is suddenly making me uncomfortable. "They probably didn't mean it. Totally. It was giving them something to do."

"Something to do?" yells Ninai. "Like writing evil e-mails to Olivia from Tyler professing his undying love? It's sick. I don't say this about too many people, but I hate anyone, I'm sorry to say, who would stoop so low."

My stomach muscles are clamping together. I walk with the phone over to the window so I can get some fresh air. That was me, in another life. That was me who wrote those pseudo love letters.

"There can be NOTHING redeeming about them," finishes Ninai.

"How soon can you come over?" I ask, trying to change the subject.

"Fifteen minutes," says Ninai.

"Twenty," says Olivia.

"Great," I say, feeling like a sellout. They are so uber wonderful, and I'm about to spoil everything by dancing with Winslow tomorrow.

Yes, tomorrow is my birthday. I guess the toilet paper can count as decorations.

Max Heeder to the Max

I don't want to wake up, but Mom is shaking me. "It's your special day," she says.

"Huh?" I say, bolting upright. I look outside the door in the hallway. It's clean. All the piled-up laundry is gone, and the carpet vacuumed.

She places her fingers to her lips. "Happy birthday, Ernestine." Oh, right. It's Friday. It's the dance. It's my birthday, December 19. After an eternity, I am fourteen.

I feel SOOOO old. I think I have aged a hundred years this past week alone. "There's a very big package for you on the table. Go look. I think it's from your father."

I pad down the hall to the kitchen, which sparkles, and is clutter-free. No more catalogs and mail stacked on the counters, no dishes in the sink, and two new gleaming pink sponges.

"I got sick of it," says Mom. "I stayed up last night cleaning and organizing. I haven't done that since . . ." Her voice trails off.

"Since Dad left," I finish.

"I got sick of being the one holding down the fort all of the time. Your father was always happy," she says quietly. "It drove me crazy that my getting mad at him didn't mean anything. I've never met anyone more unreliable." Then she clamps her hand over her mouth, breathes, and unpries her fingers from her lips. She faces me and looks me directly in the eye. "I'm sorry."

Outside, I can hear the constant drum of rain. Mom puts her arm around my shoulder, and then pushes me toward the kitchen table. "Don't just stand there. Open it up, silly."

It's a large brown paper-covered box the size of a toaster oven. Dad usually picks out THE BEST presents. But I can't say this to Mom, who prefers to make these homemade photo collages for me and stuff. I pick up the box and shake it, hoping to get a clue. It's surprisingly light. "Not books or music from Linden Tree. It's . . ." I tear off the paper.

Mom races to the kitchen drawer and hands me a scissors so I can cut the packing tape. With a few snips,

I'm able to wedge open one side. The tissue paper crinkles as I pull off the gold foil tape and uncover a little black top with hot pink spaghetti straps. It's from the Max Heeder catalog. Taffeta material, of course. The top is perfect. EXCELLENT! Exactly what I would have wanted if I could have gone to the dance as me. And there's a matching clutch bag made out of leather so fresh and soft it still moos. "It's perfect." I feel like the tissue paper is balled up in my throat.

It would look really great on me if I had thin arms, and if I were to actually go to the dance as a regular person and not wearing a very red, very ugly holiday apron stamped with a Christmas tree (Ninai will be sure to protest the lack of Kwanzaa and Hanukkah lights) and a jingle bell hat. I feel the tears coming on. "Mom, it's not fair!"

"I'm surprised. Usually, you're a little put-off by your father's extravagant designer presents. But I know how much you want to please him." She throws her flappy arms around me and envelops me to her chest. "You can still wear it."

She doesn't understanding anee-thing. "Helpers wear aprons. You hand out colas and take photos with a jingle hat on your head. Nobody will know or care what I'm wearing!"

I'm already dialing Dad's number and walking into my bedroom. I'm not going to tell him about not being able to really wear the top.

Bizarrely, Dad picks up on one ring. "Daddy, I love it. I mean, the top's great and the purse to match. You didn't have to do that."

"But I did. How often does your daughter turn fourteen? Does the top fit?"

"Yes," I say, even though I haven't tried it on. I'm actually staring at the beautiful silver tissue wrapping paper. "It's perfect."

My dad's not saying anything, so I'm wondering whether he wants me to gush more, or maybe I could try it on and give him a verbal fashion show.

"Sweet pea, there's something I've gotta tell you, okay?" Dad's voice is unusually saccharine, which makes me nervous.

"Sure, Dad." My stomach clenches and I worry that Big Lips is back. I start shredding the tissue paper in the gift box.

"It's about your b-day." He sighs into the phone. "Man, this is hard to say but I know you—my wonderful, wonderful baby girl—will understand because that's how you are. Listen, it's soooo good. I've got an interview tomorrow."

"An interview. Tomorrow? You were supposed to fly up. It's my birthday." I'm, in fact, staring at his birthday card. There's a photo of a really happy, toothy teenage girl jumping on the beach. Since when does Dad EVER mail anything in time? He's always at least two days late with some excuse and, if he was coming up to visit, he would have brought a present with him.

"Is it important?" I ask, my voice unintentionally going up into a whine. I start to pace around the room. "Did your manager finally get the financing for your movie, Dad?"

"We're close on that, Ernestine. Real close. Schuyler thinks we'll know for certain in another four to eight weeks. Maybe by Valentine's Day."

"But, Dad, isn't that what they always say?" I stop in front of the mirror, which is a big mistake because my glasses are smudgy.

"The interview," says Dad. "It's not a film thing. A marketing job for a distribution company. I'll be helping that department look at spreadsheets."

"But I thought you moved to L.A. so you could be an artist and get away from all that!" I can hear my voice rising an octave.

"It'll only be temporary. It'll be good for making

connections, and I could really use the job right now."

But what about all the money he made from Apple stocks? As if he can read my mind, he says, "Stock options aren't what they're cracked up to be, especially when you sell at the wrong time and then you invest in the wrong time. You understand don't ya? I'll make it up to you. Swear it, sweet pea."

"Yeah, Dad." I think I'm about to cry so I squeak out, "Gotta go." I hear him spurt, "Love ya," as I hang up the phone.

I meander into the living room, where Mom, who's working on the computer, glances at me with her stony gargoyle face. "What was that about? Is something wrong?"

I gaze out the window. The rain outside has slowed down to a couple of drips now. "Nothing," I say.

Forever

I remember the day I found out about our forever house. It was shortly after we moved to California and I was sitting next to my dad by his desk in our rental. The sweat beads still dotted his forehead from his bike ride, and he smelled like eucalyptus and salt. Placing his blue bike helmet on the computer desk, he went onto the Remax website. "That's going to be our new home, Taf," he had said, grabbing a bottle of water and taking a gulp. I remember staring at the flat screen and seeing a small ranch house with a door in the middle and two windows flanking it, and a white picket fence. It looked like the kind of house I might draw myself. At the time I was eleven, and not exactly a budding da Vinci.

The next week he and Mom took me to see the actual house. We drove down Burgess Drive past the Menlo Park Civic Center where Mom would take me to the library, when she used to do that sort of thing, and then we passed these small houses. Dad narrated, "Some of these houses are old railway cabooses. At least I know that the ones down by the Stanford Golf Course are. It's where the servants used to live." Then he blindfolded me and kept on driving up a hill for quite a while. I was imagining which one of those dollhouses was going to be ours. As we parked, Dad jumped out and took off my blindfold and placed his hands over my eyes.

"Dirk," said Mom. "C'mon, let her see."

"No way. It'll be more fun this way." We bounced up to the house in Sharon Heights and it seemed like we'd been walking for a while when we stopped and Dad went, "Okay, on the count of three, open them. One. Two. Three." He lifted his hands off my eyes. "Ta-da!" he shouted. "What do you think?" The house that stood in front of me was enormous, sandy-colored with a tile roof, shutters, and turrets that made it look like a castle.

"This is ours?" I began. "But, Dad, you said it was a little house with three rooms and I'd sleep in the garage."

"Dirk, you didn't." Mom swatted him with her handbag but I could tell this time she wasn't angry.

Dad grinned so big I could see his pink gums. "I was kidding with you, sweet pea. This is our house!"

"Really?"

He hugged me tight. "Really and truly."

"It's soooooo beautiful!"

"Wait till you go inside," he said, swooping me off my feet as Mom opened the door with a key. As we marched into the entrance hall, a majestic curved staircase rose to the left and a giant chandelier hung from the ceiling. From the bay window and sliders beyond the sunken living room, I could see a kidney-shaped pool with a waterfall and sliding board inset into rock.

"Can we stay here forever?" I asked.

Dad's arms tightened around me. "Forever," he said, "and that's a promise."

The Day

La Cambia Middle School
8th-Grade Holiday Festival

December 19

Period 6 1:15-2:47

Place C-4 C-5 E1 E2 E3 E4

Activity: All Students must be signed up for their activities on or before December 7. Any student not registered will be placed into an activity.

<u>Activity</u>

Ropes team C-4

Ornament making E-4

Art projects E-3

Bingo E-9

Holiday Card Making C-1

La Cambia Middle School

"Where Success Is Expected"

Yes, it's definitely Friday, the last day of school before Winter Break, the day of the dance and MY BIRTHDAY, and, in an attempt to cheer me up, I'm being forced to play Bingo against my will. It's a party day at school in every class, even in Stuckley's English class. So far I only have B-9 covered on my little board.

Olivia keeps staring at Winslow, who's playing some scary fantasy board game with Sneed. He's still dressing like Mr. Prep and his hair is almost crew cut–short. You'd think that would freak her out a little. I mean Olivia only has nineteenth-century Russian peasant or medieval clothes in her wardrobe. Wouldn't she think that Winslow dressing so normal would be a little strange? No, apparently not. I think she believes that he's styling and grooming because of her. She actually calls over to him, "I hear you're going to be at the dance."

Winslow, the prep, who today is in a blue polo shirt, palms a goblin action figure. "Yup, most definitely. Because *someone* I know will be there." He gestures with his chin over at Petra. NOOOOO!

I start talking fast. "Yes, like me, Ninai, and Olivia. It'll be quite the crew."

He's smirking. "Yup." Olivia turns to me with a big-time happy look. She thinks he's coming because of her.

All at once, I'm thinking about how I'm going

to have to dance with Winslow in front of Olivia, even if it is just one time. Sure, I've thought about it before, but now the reality is really hitting me. My heart dives and is eaten by my gut. I must think of something to tell Olivia, to prepare her. But it's not going to be easy. She's showing me her small crooked teeth because she's actually smiling. "Soon you'll be able to see the results of my powers and see me dazzle Winslow, my own private Boris. *Da?*"

"Yeah," I say. "I'm going as one of Santa's little helpers."

A cluster of teachers are talking and drinking their energy drinks, which is making them a little too wired and loud. Some of the girls are wearing Santa hats with bells on them so whenever they raise their hands the hats jingle. Groups of guys, like Tyler and Justin, have brought their footballs. Sneed and Winslow keep on playing with their elf warriors and troll princess figurines.

Ms. Stuckley runs her fingers through her spiky hair and calls out I-6 in her pseudo British voice. Olivia leans into me and rolls her eyes. "I can't wait to see The Girls pulling up in their enviro-friendly limo."

Ninai twirls her fingers in the air. "How many miles do you think the Hummer thing gets per gallon? One?" She pretends to stick a finger down her throat and gag.

Then Ninai cups her mouth, whispering something to Olivia and both of them turn their bodies away from me.

Uh-oh. Could they know somehow that I'm planning on dancing with Winslow and hurting Olivia? NOT that I want to, but I HAVE to. I can't stand seeing them whisper. It's so un-them and so me. I sidle over, "So, what are you guys talking about?"

Ninai swats her hand in front of her face. "Oh, the usual. The administration totally ignoring everything we've worked so hard to accomplish this past year. I'm just so upset about the decorations. I've told Mrs. Barnes a thousand times that the dance should celebrate winter in a nondenominational kind of way. It's apparently oh so hard to follow the Constitution. I'm definitely cooking up a letter to write to the school board."

Olivia bites a strand of her hair and looks disturbingly dreamy.

"Are you upset about Santa hats or is it something else?" I fish.

Ninai points to the reindeer on the bulletin board. "How about the fact that there're going to be a bazillion

Christmas decorations, a couple of dreidels, but only one symbol of Kwanzaa, and Muslims, well, they don't exist nor does any other religion or practice."

Wow. "I thought you might have also been mad about something else. Never mind," I say, as I see Ms. Stuckley spinning the plastic bingo ball thingie.

As if Olivia knows what I'm thinking, she puts her hand on my shoulder, and looks at me all reassuringly. I smile but my insides twist. Yes, I'm going to be the uber backstabber. It seems like a good time to give Olivia and Ninai their Christmas—I mean holiday—presents, since Olivia is agnostic but believes in the possibility of a higher power and Ninai celebrates Hanukah, Christmas, and all of the Filipino holidays. "Here," I say, handing each of them a little robin's-egg blue tissue paper bundle. "It's not anything big but . . ."

Ninai unwraps hers first. "I love it, Ern." She pulls out a beige rock, which is the size of a golf ball, only cut in half. Olivia unwraps an identical looking rock. On the outside, the stones are plain, almost concrete-y looking but on the inside they're rose crystal. "I love it," says Ninai. "Absolutely gorgeous."

"Da," adds Olivia. "Beautiful. They feel so cool and reassuring. Like the first rain."

"I have this thing about crystals." I point to the one in Ninai's hand. "I bought it at a shop, but someday I hope to find them myself."

"I'm indebted to you forever," says Olivia. "We're giving you your birthday-slash-holiday present at the dance." But I'm not really listening. I'm watching Petra and Caylin go on about the limo.

Ninai covers another square with her bingo piece. Until this moment, I had totally forgotten that we are all supposed to be actually playing bingo. She's one away from winning. "Ernestine," she says, watching me stare at The Girls, "don't think about what they did or listen to their dumb plans. Stop thinking about how much you hate them for everything they've done."

How surreal my life is, how Dada. The jingle-bell-girl hats continue to tinkle. "In my opinion, The Girls really need to be taken down a couple of notches." Is this really me talking?

"N-twenty," says Ms. Stuckley.

"BINGO!" shouts Ninai.

Primping

After school, it's a miracle but I convince Olivia and Ninai to ride our bikes into downtown Palo Alto to go shopping. Every other day, when I asked them if they wanted to ride their bikes or do anything physical, they always came up with a good excuse. It's pretty safe because of all the bike lanes, but you have to look out for the retired dot-comers who think they're training for the Tour de France. Santa Cruz Avenue is all done up in lights and wreaths and I can't help thinking from Ninai's perspective how Christmas-centered everything looks. Olivia introduces me to a thrift store, where she gets all of her outfits. A thrift store. Wow, I've really become my mom. There are racks and racks of tops, all coordinated by color but not by size. Plastic bags full of socks and assorted mismatched Christmas cards are in boxes, and there are items such as children's books, record albums, glass juicers, and shot glasses with Empire State Buildings and Elvis Presleys stacked on shelves.

"Whoa," I say, "I had NO idea. I'm serious. Look at this stuff!" Outside, a red-and-blue bus with an ad for the Stanford Shopping Center chugs by. But for once I'm not missing full-price retail shopping.

Ninai eyes me suspiciously as the speakers blare "Rudolph." "You act as if you've never been here before, Ernestine."

That's just it. I swallow hard. "Guess I'm seeing it with new eyes."

B-day, D-day

"There's something I've got to talk to you about," Mom says as she Velcros her photography equipment into her black carrying case to take to the dance.

I look her right in the eye. "I know. Dad's not coming. He can't make it up for my birthday because he has a job interview and his film blah blah blah. The usual pathetic excuse."

Mom stops and blinks. "When you called him, he told you, right?"

I bite my bottom lip. "Yup."

She reaches for my arm. "I'm *so* sorry, Little Love."

"Do you think his film's ever going to be optioned?"

Mom stares at her photography equipment and shrugs. "Who knows. Anything is possible."

"I seriously doubt it." But I think I know of a good screenplay for Dad. One that might be interesting enough to actually get made. I'll tell it to him, to both of them, sometime. But not right here. Not right now.

"Are you upset, Ernestine?"

I shake my head. "Disappointed, maybe, but that's nothing new." I love my dad. I do, but he wasn't there for me all the time. Not the way my mom was. I mean, she has been gone a lot with her photography stuff, but I know in a pinch she'd come through.

Mom fingers the strap to her camera that's around her neck. "I think we should start a new, totally honest relationship now that you're fourteen." She takes a deep breath. "And I'm getting myself together. Look, I never want to poison you against your father. He loves you very much, as much as he loves anybody."

"I know," I say.

"The truth is I've gotten so used to pulling your father's weight that I lied about him paying for things sometimes. Originally, he said he was going to pay for half of your expenses but then things got tight for him. So he promised if I fronted the money now he'd pay for things later, but you know your dad." She sighs.

"So he's been cheating you?" I feel nauseous. "Why didn't you tell me?"

"You look up to him. I don't want to get in the way of your relationship with your dad. But I'd like to work on ours. I think we should spend more time together," she says, tapping her fingers on the camera stand. "I'm excited about photographing your dance. I'm so glad that Tosh suggested it."

I raise my eyebrows. Why does she have to remind me that she's flaky enough to take advice from a medium named Tosh?

But I don't comment. I don't *whatever* her. I just see this middle-aged woman who's really excited, her cheeks all flushed, and I smile and feel all butter-popcorn happy that she's looking forward to something, and then I throw my arms around MY BIG-MOUTH mother. "I love you." I hug her with all my might. "Next time, be honest with me. I'm sorry if I've said things or was embarrassed by you. It's something I'm working on."

"I'm proud of you." She curls a piece of hair around my ear, and I let her.

Santa's Little Helper

So I go to Winterfest early, as a slave. I'm sorry, did I say that? I meant as one of the many happy leadership helpers conscripted into the status-quo army. As I stroll into the gym, Maggie the Mushroom, with her important clipboard under her arm, wearing a jingle bell hat, hands me a red—yes, red—and shiny polyester apron and a hat to match that I apparently have to wear, which completely blocks out the coolness of my outfit. But even though I'm registering on the decent scale, I don't register with Mushroom. She slaps a number on my back, HELPER #9. I want to choke the self-important smile off her face as she directs me to refreshment-girl duty.

"Where're Caylin and Petra?" I ask, trying to prepare myself for having to deal with them next.

Mushroom crosses something off her clipboard. "They asked me to set this up for them since they'll be coming to the dance later. In their Hummer." Correction: *my* Hummer. But I'm not so sure it was the most fabulous pick after all since they guzzle just a little too much fuel.

On refreshment-girl duty, I arrange rows of paper cups of cola and orange soda. As I'm throwing chocolate-chip cookies on reindeer napkins, Olivia and Ninai amble into the gym. Ninai stares at the strings of white lights framing the gym, the enormous pink and yellow snowflakes taped to black paper, and sticks her finger down her throat. Then when she sees the skating snowman scene next to the fake gift boxes in front of the fake fire and fake stockings she pretends to retch. Olivia pantomines cleaning up the mess, and

I begin to giggle. The decorations really are lame.

Olivia pushes her hair out of her eyes and smiles at me. "You look exactly like Santa's little helper."

"Thanks," I say, *ho ho ho*ing. "I had no choice."

"But we did," says Ninai. "We made sure not to follow orders." She taps the cutesy poster in the gym.

Holiday Spirit Day
December 19
You must wear red AND green if you are participating in
La Cambia Middle School Leadership

Watching The Leadership Girls all Christmas-ed out to the max, Olivia shakes her head.

"What if you only wear red with no green?" says Olivia. "Then you are apparently SUCH a nonconformist. Maybe even a Communist."

"Or green," says Ninai. "That would also be out there. Liberal, Green Party–type, no doubt."

I put my arms around Olivia and Nina. "That's why we are wearing black." Olivia is dressed in nice bikerish boots, and a flowy top that fits her really well. She looks almost hot in a Russian/medieval combo, and Ninai has a flowery dress that makes her look almost romantic. I convinced them that we needed to put in some girl time to get ready for the dance.

"Here," says Olivia, thrusting a present in front of me. "For you, Erneski. Happy Birthday!"

"It's from both of us," says Ninai. "But before you open that we have another present. Well, not really a present. More like a pledge. We'll even go on another bike ride with you. But no big hills."

"I promise." I carefully pull the tissue paper off the present so nothing tears.

"I'm aging," says Ninai and helps me rip the paper. I open the box. It's a scarf with an *E* written on it with gold ink.

"I did it with a special fabric calligraphy pen," Olivia says, her lips curled up in a smile. The scarf is aqua and purple with gold flecks, and it's so ugly it's almost cool.

"Thanks," I say. "It's really amazing that you did this." I tie it around my neck.

"And we have one more present," says Olivia, rather mysteriously, which isn't unusual for her since she lives to be mysterious.

"Okay," I say, putting out my hand.

"Nope," says Ninai. "You'll just have to wait for the right moment."

"Okay, then I'll just have to wait." I act as if waiting is no big deal, but I love presents of all kinds and it kills me, KILLS me to wait, so I decide to take my mind off my impatience by showing off.

Since Mushroom has her back to me, I take off my apron for a minute. "Ta-da!" Olivia and Ninai nod approvingly. I'm wearing my Max Heeder top, wedge sandals, red sweater, and a pair of 1970s jeans I picked up at the thrift store, and I look good. And my hair, although not silky, flows down my back going in every direction and looks not frizzy, but curly, wavy, and interesting, like you can't tell what each strand is going to do. And for the first time in a long time, I applied a little mascara and some blush. I almost looked like the old me, except that in this version of my life I'm Ernestine, friend of Olivia and Ninai and almost-pal of Winslow.

Ninai nods approvingly and Olivia spins around me. "You look *vonderful*, Ernestine. *Da!*"

"Thanks," I say, smiling at Olivia and Ninai. "You guys look good too."

Mushroom and Invisible Girl hustle up to me, pointing at the refreshment table. Mushroom Girl is armed with a megaphone.

"I better go play slave to the Leadership Nazis. Otherwise, they'll bring out their megaphone and whack me with it," I say, putting my apron back on.

Ninai waves her hand in front of her face. "Not the megaphone. Please go."

I'm not sure exactly how I'm going to cut out of my server duties and find Winslow, but that's my challenge.

I go back to the cookies and sodas and pretend to line everything up. But I'm really just standing there like an idiot, waiting for Winslow to arrive with Petra in the limo.

The gym doors officially open. The dance begins. As the crowds blast through the door, I hear lots of applauding and whistling and voices screaming, "LIMO!"

The Girls are back in town.

Bummer Hummer

A stretch Hummer pulls up to the curb in front of the gym. A husky driver with a little black cap and goatee hops out and opens the door.

I crane my neck to see Caylin being helped out of the seat. She's holding a digital camera and takes a picture of herself. They have the limo driver take pictures. There's more whistling. Then Petra prances out dressed up so much like Caylin you'd think they'd been cloned.

How pathetic to work that hard to get attention. With a gas-guzzling limo? C'mon.

I think back to how I should be there with them, and, suddenly, I feel all muddled and mixed up. How can I really scoff? It was my idea. It's my birthday. I try to imagine what the inside looks like, all stocked with Pringles, dry-roasted nuts, Fruit Roll-Ups, and energy drinks. Pressing my face up against the mirror reflected glass, I'd be able to see out but nobody would be able to see in and they'd all be wondering who was inside. Of course, we would pop our heads out of the sunroof and shriek. The music would be turned up full-blast to our favorite songs. It would just be me and The Girls together, best friends, doing up my birthday. Then, after the dance, we would go to eat at Benihana.

But The Girls don't even look at me. I'm now just Snack Girl.

And wait a minute. Where's Winslow?

My One Shot

Music blasts from two giant speakers. The DJ, with earphones on, bops his head to the beat. The wall behind him is framed by blue, yellow, red, and green lights. A song booms: "It's a good day! I want to be just like you. I want to be you!" I tense up, thinking about anyone actually wanting to be like someone else.

Petra, Caylin, and their acolytes rush into the gym screaming like they've just won a make-out contest with their favorite celebrity. They're holding hands and drinking Cokes. So far there's very little dancing going on. The light shines on all the jewelry. There's lots of jumping and hugging going on with The Girls. Didn't they just see one another in school? Most of them loop arm-in-arm and run straight to the wall to read the dance-gram messages written on little stars, moons, and snowflakes. Some pull their friends so hard they almost trip.

I'm still standing guard over the refreshment stand when my mother, with a camera slung around her neck, bounds up to me. "Having fun?" she asks.

I can't answer this question. This is not how my birthday was supposed to turn out.

Mom holds her camera focused on me and starts snapping. "Smile! You look gorgeous."

"Please," I say. "Can you take pictures of me later?"

She gazes around at all of the kids bunched up with their friends, nodding their heads to the music, which is really rocking. "Sure, honey." She winks, as she heads toward the wall with the dance grams. "I'll give you some space."

Space. I don't need space. Winslow needs space and I need Winslow! Where is he? Is he outside with the rest of the boys? Finally, Tyler and Justin move into the gym and the rest of the sheep follow. I look to see if Winslow is among them.

I see a guy with longish hair and my heart flutters. Oh, right. He cut his hair. The suck-up. Where's Winslow? Petra hugs Caylin, who bounces and swishes her hair. She's wearing tight jeans, a black jacket with a lacy, frilly shirt underneath that's way too cropped to be a top. Justin has his hands on Caylin's waist. She keeps on pretending to bump into Petra and Tyler. Is she trying, in her way, to get some distance from Justin? Then Petra turns around and sneers at me in my apron. It's like she has eyes on the back of her highlighted hair.

Petra motions at Olivia to come onto the dance floor. Pointing to Tyler's back, she smacks her lips like he wants Olivia to dance. She's acting out those fake e-mails we wrote from Tyler to Oliva. This is too much. How can Petra do this again? Not that Olivia is falling for it this time. Tyler's sort of rocking out in his laid-back way, swinging his head to the beat. Is Petra trying to get Olivia to dance with him, and, then, like, what—spit in her face? In the distance, I can see Mom motioning to a bunch of kids to smile for her camera. To look all happy.

I can't take this anymore. Everyone else in the room stands in girl and boy packs. Someone turns off all the lights and some girls shriek. The lights go back on. Two sixth-grade boys pretend to punch each other while their buddies chase and bump into everyone.

"Don't forget," says the DJ, who's all decked-out in holiday gear, "Santa's in the house. He's wearing a jingle bell hat."

The crowd cheers, and I'm thinking, *Okay, where's Winslow?* As Ninai and Olivia whisper in the bleachers, I can tell they're thinking the same thing. *Where's Winslow?* Olivia's actually pushed her hair out of her eyes and is surveying the room. Then I glimpse Olivia and Ninai huddled together whispering, and something about their glances in my direction lets me know they're talking about me. I don't like it one bit.

"Yesterday, at some other school called Oakview, they were much louder," says the DJ, naming our rival school.

"Booo, booo," goes the crowd and there's not one big blond dude among the bunch. But he promised he'd be here. Maybe I missed him somehow.

"When they booed you, they were MUCH louder!" calls out the DJ.

"Boo! BOOO!" goes the crowd, a decibel louder.

"Boo? What is this, a Halloween party?" asks the DJ.

There's dancing now, mostly groups of girls. "Everybody dance! C'mon!" screams the DJ.

When's Winslow getting here? Why wasn't he in that Hummer?

Girls give girls piggyback rides, which turns into boys giving girls piggyback rides, which turns into girls giving boys piggyback rides.

"Time to wind down, and hook up with a slow dance," says the DJ. "Listen to your heart."

The gym thins out, and the couples appear from the periphery and fill out the dance floor. After another survey, I see that Winslow is definitely not among the couples converging onto the floor. He's definitely not the VERY short boy with the tall girl. They're swaying, their arms around each other. Only preppy leadership girls and the couples are out there. I see Petra stepping out with Justin. Certainly, Winslow should have been here by now. Everyone else watches, including me. There are a bunch of girls doing a group slow dance.

After the song ends, Petra goes back with her

friends by the wall of dance gram messages. I hear her laughing. "Thank god that dweeb didn't show up. Even if he's looking semidecent."

"He still might."

"I don't think so. Not after what I did to him." Then they high-five.

It hits me like a rockslide, splits me like an earthquake, and drowns me like a flood.

Winslow isn't coming.

It's amazingly unfair. I'm punished, while Petra gets to celebrate after she cheated. I mean, nothing seems to have happened to her, and it's been more than twenty-four hours. Suddenly, I need to cry. I can't do it in front of THEM. They are about to pass this way. It's just too much. I race down the hallway, past all of the signs for the dance and the outside picnic tables, and find a bathroom that's far away from the blaring music and from them, my so-called friends.

Inside the bathroom, I let everything out and, after washing my face, stare at the mirror at my red eyes, my flyaway hair. I blot my cheeks with a paper towel, not even bothering to reapply lip gloss or whatever. What's the point? I look at my watch. Eighty minutes left of the dance. *He could still show,* I think. *Give it some time.* So I lean over the sink, my hands on the cold porcelain counting to one hundred Mississippi. I am at ninety-seven Mississippi when I hear screams.

Not Silly!

I rush outside. The sounds are coming from the parking area. By the limo. It's covered with shaving cream and Silly String.

Shallow! Cheaters! Hate me!

The words are sprayed on the windshield and on the trunk and hood. I just don't get it. Silly String. Toilet paper. That's Petra and Caylin's (and my) handiwork. They wouldn't do it to themselves. Beside the car, a straw dummy dressed in mule heels, a tank, and jeans, leans against the bumper.

Caylin and Petra stand outside with a growing crowd that includes the limo driver, the principal, Mrs. Barnes on a crackly walkie-talkie, and two teachers. The Girls are clutching their chests as if the straw girl is like a voodoo doll with pins through its heart.

Petra points to me. "She did it," she says simply.

Principal Barnes stares at me incredulously. "Ernestine?"

"No," I say, backing away. "Sorry. Wasn't me."

"She did just leave the snack table," says a voice in the crowd. It sounds like Mushroom.

I turn around. Yes, it's her, frowning at me with her porcini hair. "I was in the bathroom!"

"Oh, yeah," Mushroom goes, "but you were gone a looooong time."

"I went to the other bathroom. I just needed a break. From the dance. And . . ." I take a deep breath. "Don't stick up for them." I point to The Girls. "Do you know what they think of you? They call you Maggie the Mushroom, and you"—I nod over at her friend—"Invisible Girl. Get a life. Dress how you want." Maggie shakes her head and rolls her eyes at Meshell-like-the-beach.

Petra juts her jaw out and stares at me like I'm mono and bird flu all rolled together. "In the gym yesterday, she screamed a psychotic threat that something bad would happen to me today."

"She completely did," adds Caylin.

"I said something bad would happen to Petra because . . . because," I say, sputtering, "I was trying to warn her." How lame I sound.

I'm so far from myself I've forgotten how to react normally, like I don't even protest when Mrs. Barnes starts printing my name on some sort of pink slip for Supreme NP. She's coming down extra hard on me, I know, since I was basically on probation due to the letting-Petra-cheat-off-me incident. Looking at my watch, I see it's already 7:55. The dance will end in a little over an hour now. How can I right this wrong? Will I have to wait until another dance, which won't happen until next year? By then will I even remember I want to be Taffeta? Do I even want to be Taffeta now?

Mrs. Barnes gazes at her pink slip on her clipboard. "We'll need to go to the office and call your mother. To pick you up pronto from this dance."

"That's unnecessary," I say. "Since she's here. Taking photos."

"Last I saw she was over by the DJ taking some close-ups," says Caylin.

Mrs. Barnes talks into her walkie-talkie. "Please bring Ernestine's mother to my office. She's over by the DJ."

Suddenly, I see a hennaed hair vision whip past me. "I did it, Mrs. Barnes," says Olivia, racing up the sidewalk, almost falling down. "I messed up the limo. Caylin and Petra had it coming to them for what they did to Ernestine." As Ninai speeds up next to her on the curb, Olivia lists on her fingers. "Cheating off her,

TP'ing her house. It's our supreme birthday present." I'm trying to take this in. *Olivia did this? Medieval Russian Queen? And my friend. Yes, my friend!*

"Sorry not to say anything, but I couldn't tell you," she adds in a low whisper. So that's what she and Ninai had been whispering about for the past few days.

My mind leafs through all of the incidents from last year, and I remember the fake e-mails that we—chiefly I—wrote to Olivia pretending to be from Tyler.

Mrs. Barnes stands there, blinking like she can't believe that I didn't do this.

"I don't care what you do to me. It was worth it," says Olivia, looking at Mrs. Barnes. "Petra cheated and Ernestine got punished. I can't stand it anymore." Ninai is nodding her head.

I stand there silent, completely ashamed.

"Put me on NP, give *me* a suspension," Olivia cries out, catching the principal's eye. "I made the straw dummy. The writing on the limo. Let Ernestine go."

No Show

Olivia's on NP and Winslow isn't going to show up at Winterfest because Petra told him that she had NO intention of actually dancing with him. I'm having *such* a great time. The disco lights spin and the throbbing bass squeezes into my temples. Headache. I've got to get to Winslow. I'm looking at the clock. There's fifty-five minutes left of the dance. Seven to ten minutes to pedal to his house and back. Not much time. I have no choice.

I hop onto Mom's bicycle built for two and hope for the best.

Hard Knocks

After passing the thousandth blue Dumpster in front of another house in the middle of a remodel, I speed it to Winslow's. There's a very important gate around Winslow's house so I leap off my bike and, somehow, I scale the fence, scratching my legs but landing on my feet. Now I'm at the door. I bang a brass lion's head and ring the bell. Nobody comes to the door. Not his hot corporate mom or shooting-particles-down-a-mile-long-tube dad.

I go to leave when I notice that the garage door is slightly ajar, so I slither under it and push myself into a bowl of wet cat food. Gross. I have to do this, though. The lights are off and I grope around looking for a switch. Finding none, I push open the door into a hallway with a laundry room and cubbies filled with shoes. Suddenly, I feel like an idiot (and a burglar). What if his parents are home? What will they think? What could I possibly say? Soon I'm in an enormous kitchen. There's a light on above the oven and I can make out a granite countertop, cherrywood cabinets, and gleaming stainless steel appliances.

When I hear footsteps, I hold my breath, ducking next to the kitchen island that stores carving boards and a wooden block full of knives.

Now I can hear someone padding into the adjacent dining room, and I go to call out *Who's there?* when I hear a whoosh of air and a yelp of pain. A cat screeches as the butcher block falls down and knives clatter onto the tile floor.

"Who's there?" I yell.

"OWWWW," somebody moans—a voice I recognize—and another moan.

I flick on overhead lights that are on a dimmer switch by the fridge.

It's Winslow. His hair, although still short, looks almost messy. His T-shirt is black. This one says COEXIST. No polo shirt, no clean, pressed pair of khaki pants. The duct-taped shoes are back. Even the chain is back. It's ridiculous but I've never been so happy to hear clanging metal in my life.

"My hand's bleeding," he says. "I think one of the knives scraped it when it fell." He lifts up his head to gaze at me. "What are you doing here?" he demands, totally out of breath.

"I came to get you to go to Winterfest."

"Heard of knocking?"

"I did."

"Oh, riiiiight," he says, pulling off his iPod. "I thought you were . . . whatever. So I used my tae kwon do moves on the butcher block. Defensively, of course. You're lucky you weren't hurt. Yesterday, I crushed Tyler in my sparring class."

"You crushed Tyler?"

"Yeah, we're in tae kwon do together. He's been trying to build up his confidence after his, you know, the kidnapping thing last year."

I'm so surprised I blurt, "Why would Tyler need to build up his confidence? He took care of those guys, the ones that broke into his house."

Winslow scratches his chin where his love patch used to be. "Actually, Ty opened the door to the crawl space in his parents' closet and escaped under the house. The scar on his chin—you know, the one that kinda looks like a caterpillar—is from when he banged into something in the crawl space. He was really scared. He started taking tae kwon do to get over the fear thing. I've been trying to help him."

"You?" Now it's *my* turn to almost knock into the counter.

"Shocking, I know. Ever since I got my black belt I've been helping the dojo and, sometimes, Ty even comes over to my house for some pointers." He taps his black, scrubby notebook. "I write down all of the forms we're working on and some sparring class techniques in here." *Ooooh, that's why he's obsessed with that notebook.* "Plus, I'm trying to learn some Korean. I want to know more than Kibon, Taegeuk, and Palge. Which are forms."

"It sounds cool but I'm not sure if I get it," I say, being completely honest.

"Neither do I sometimes, which is the point," says Winslow. Running his hand under the faucet to wash off the little bit of blood, he laughs. "So luckily for you, I hit the cutting board." Winslow shrugs.

"I guess," I say and we laugh a little. "Your hand's still bleeding. Maybe you should put on a Band-Aid."

The Dance

Winslow blinks and I can see in his Saturn eyes how he's not going to going to give any cues for me to continue talking, like, *Yes, I'd love to hear anything you have to say.* Nope, he's going to stand there in the kitchen and force me into blurtation.

I breathe deeply and try to ignore the fact that my whole body feels like it's revved up. "Okay," I say.

"Are you disappointed?" I ask. "That I'm not Petra?"

He gazes down at his duct-taped shoes. "No, relieved, actually. I dunno. I wanted to believe, I guess. But I'd much rather be sitting here talking with a real person. I'm sorry I asked you to, you know, cheat. That was pretty heinous of me. But not you, you're pretty perfect."

His eyes flick up to my eyes, and my whole body seems to flutter for a moment. That's when I notice he's got Scotch Tape wrapped around all of his fingers. "I thought you were going to put on a Band-Aid."

"Works for me," says Winslow. "Now here's *my* question. Why are you so obsessed with getting *me* to the dance? You sound stressed."

With my foot, I trace a plank of wood. "I have to get you to dance. For a very good reason . . ." My back is up against the sink. "I had to get you to dance with me because I need to become my real self."

"Which is?"

Oh, god. Here it goes. "This beautiful, popular

girl named Taffeta Smith. Ring a bell?"

Winslow fingers his iPod and I'm feeling stupid. "You don't believe me, do you? You think I'm a mess."

He stares at me. "Wow, okay, I'm processing this." He shakes his head. "*Vous êtes un lunatic*. Did you know that means, you are . . . ?"

"Crazy!" My breath comes out in short puffs. "I can understand that."

"Crazy. That's not a bad thing but, okay, I am tripping here a little." I start to turn away. But Winslow touches my arm. "Don't go, dummy. I want to see where you're going with all of this. Taffeta—that's a kind of material. Silk. *La soie.* Sounds better in French."

"Listen to me, Winslow. I'm not joking around. Okay! This is not some attempt to get your attention. I used to be her. Taffeta. I turned into this other person." I pat my face. "Ernestine. I need to dance with you. Got it?"

He crunches his eyes at me, and moves his head side to side. "So you're telling me you used to be somebody else? Seriously?"

"YES!"

"Okay, chill. I'm not judging. I'm listening. It's not your run-of-the-mill statement like *I once broke my elbow when I was seven*. But I'm intrigued. I always wanted to be able to shapeshift into something else and get all powerful." He makes a muscle. "But you're saying you were—"

"Beautiful." I pull on my polyester apron. "Everyone used to love me. EVERYONE. They just worshipped me. I could make them do whatever I wanted. The limo thing. That was my idea because it's MY birthday today."

"When you say *everyone* worshipped, do you mean *me*?"

"Especially you."

As he pulls off his glasses to wipe them, a lopsided grin spreads over his face. "I knew it. I knew something was up with you. 'Cause you've been acting a little weird." For a moment, I'm hurt, but then Winslow crouches down. His eyes crinkle up and his lips tug into a slight smile. "Did you know there are two kinds of forces? If we didn't have gravity, we would have been pulled into the sun and would've been fried, but the two forces even things out and keep things going into orbit. Shows the importance of balancing. Don't want to get sucked up by one force or the other." Pretending to battle a force, he sways back and forth.

I blink, not sure where he's going but I'm hoping it's someplace decent. Finally, he stops his mock combat. "I bet it's hard sometimes to know who you really are," Winslow says in a whisper.

And I realize something. He's taking me seriously. He's, maybe, believing me.

Grovel

We pedal back to school on my bicycle built for two, up the long hill and into the La Cambia parking lot. I look at my cell phone. There's still twenty minutes left of the dance. YES!

As we walk through the open double gym doors, Winslow stretches out his arm. I think he's going to grab me and dance. This is it. Instead, his fingers play with the bracelet on my wrist.

"There's a lot more to you than I thought. . . ."

"What did you think?" I'm hanging on his every word, watching the door for Olivia. He is still twisting the bracelet around my wrist.

"I don't know," he says, smiling. "That you're really cute when you get all weird and babbly."

"Do you believe me?" I ask. "Tell me. Be honest now."

"I believe that *you* believe," he says.

His fingers are still touching my wrist, and I'm finding it hard to concentrate, to make my words stick together into a sentence. "I know I was Taffeta. It's not a belief."

"Okay," he says. "I'm open to new ideas. Sure. Because, I seriously believe I might have been King Arthur, Lancelot, or maybe just the Round Table itself."

I want to be mad at him for not really believing me, but I'm too jumbled. "What do you think of me? I mean, why was it so hard until recently for us to connect?"

"I don't know." He smiles and drops my wrist. It's hard to hear because of the music. "I guess I thought sometimes that you didn't approve of me." He shrugs his shoulders. "I'm not exactly on time with assignments. Don't follow directions. You and Olivia and Ninai always hand everything a week ahead of time."

"But you get an A on every test. Everything!"

"Yeah. But not on my report card. Too many incompletes. I can't stand to do every little thing the teacher says. All of the hoops we have to jump through and sometimes you seem like you're playing the game, that's all. You're like a Girl Scout."

Me, like a Girl Scout? I laugh at the idea. But maybe it was true now. "So you thought I was judging you."

"Judging everyone, in fact."

"Yeah. Maybe I was." I smile—judging people is a trait Ernestine seems to share with Taffeta. "Maybe I do," I admit, wishing he'd start playing with my bracelet again.

"But you're a freak. Like me."

"Yeah. I guess."

He takes off his glasses to rub his eyes. They're big and fringed with lashes. Thick like a girl's, but I can see that when he grows into his body that, well, he'd be sort of interesting-looking.

A fast song ends and a slow song comes on.

"Want to dance?" he asks.

I hear his words. I mean, I know Winslow has said them, but somehow it seems surreal.

Like I've been waiting ALL THIS TIME for this moment and now it's here and it's just us.

My Moment

That's all. It's like the rest of the kids and the teachers aren't there. And somehow I thought there would be more of a drumroll. Like a giant highlighter pen would come down from the sky and highlight us in blue and everyone would stop what they were doing and watch and nod approvingly. But it's not like that at all. It's much more private and normal, like it was just an extension of any kind of moment we would have had together. My body plays catch-up and, suddenly, I feel like my insides have dragged down into my toes.

"You look good," Winslow shouts over the music.

Okay, me, the lights, the DJ equipment—we're all one because I'm totally and completely electrified. I'm about to actually go onto the dance floor.

Winslow is reaching out to grab my hand, not my bracelet. It's going to happen. My dance with Winslow that will change me back. Out of the corner of my eye, I see Olivia. She's still standing with Principal Barnes, who has a walkie-talkie up to her ear. She stood up for me and acted like a true friend. Olivia thought it wasn't fair that I got punished. She could have let me take the fall. Yes, she's a *very* good friend.

As Winslow's arms go around my waist, Olivia twists her body around to stare at me and Winslow. Her mouth drops open and her eyes blink a few times, and there is no magic fluttering of her fingers now.

What am I doing?

Not Me!

I can see that Olivia is making the connection. Me being so helpful. Me giving advice to her about Winslow. All of those *but I only want to help you*s—I can tell she's not buying it this time. Even from the corner of the gym, I can see her mouth forming a round *o*, then twisting into a scowl of disgust.

I bolt, leaving Winslow on the dance floor by himself, and rush over to Olivia. "It's not how it looks."

"Winslow's arms were around your waist," she says matter-of-factly.

"No! Well, yes." *How do I say this?* "It wasn't like he was going to kiss me or something. He wanted to dance and I told him that I didn't want to dance. He thought you went away. Because of the incident. To the principal's office."

"No, he didn't. Don't lie to me."

"He probably thought I was you or something. It's dark in here. All those lights." I squint and shield myself from the strobes.

Winslow trots over to us. "See . . . he's coming to see *you*, not me," I say. "Go dance with him." I point her toward the dance floor.

"You of such short memory." She shoots me a

reproving look. "Mrs. Barnes, as in the principal, said I'm on NP. I have to wait here until my parents come pick me up." Mrs. Barnes is in fact, conveniently, standing next to the refreshment stand helping herself to a few cookies. She must need lots of sugar to make it through her job.

I swallow and yell, "Principal Barnes. The Hummer and straw girl—I was the one who did it. The messing up the LIMO! Olivia only said she did it to cover up for me!"

Then I drag her over to Winslow and shove her toward him. He glances over at me, giving me a shocked, questioning look. *What?* he mouths and I feel a twinge of guilt. I can tell he's confused, just like me. I mean my mind is pretzeled, but I know one thing. I can't do this again to Olivia, to somebody who trusted me and has been my friend. But this is tough, because I also really don't want to hurt Winslow, either. It seems I have no choice.

"Forget it," I say. "Olivia likes you. NOT ME! I wouldn't dance with you unless forced, like in a desert island–type situation." Winslow furrows his brow and lifts his head back like he wants to spit at me, like he's realizing for the first time that I'm actually, really and truly insane. And maybe I am, losing my one chance to be myself.

Olivia is fingering the buttons on Winslow's digital *Star Wars* watch. "Can I communicate with Han Solo?" she asks, playfully. Is that lip gloss making her mouth so shiny? "I want to speak to someone from the Rebel Command Center," she goes on, rather dimly. Is she playing dumb to get close to Winslow? *It's working,* she mouths. And then it hits me. I was the one who told her to try flirting, being silly, and using an excuse for epidermis contact. It was all *my* fault, and Winslow doesn't seem to be minding in the least. Nope, he likes having his buttons literally pushed, and Olivia's hennaed hair in his face.

Suddenly, he looks at me and shakes his head, and I can see that he's disgusted with me, but he's a boy, and he wraps his arms around Olivia and spins her and she laughs and they're having a great time, and it's like I'm not even there at all. Okay, he looks up at me once, maybe twice, and scowls, maybe more, but mostly I have my head down because I don't want to see the confusion, the hurt in his eyes. Part of me wants Winslow to fight for me, to run after me, but mostly I'm relieved because I just want to sit down on the bleachers and stare at my hands for a while.

Ninai is clapping—she's so happy Olivia finally got to dance with Winslow.

I feel good about what I have done but for some reason I'm shaking so badly that I stumble toward the bleachers to sit down. As Mrs. Barnes pulls me into her office, all I can think about is that I'm now really and truly and always locked into Ernestine.

NO!

A hand pulls me along out of the dance, through the foyer. "Do you realize how serious this is?" asks Mrs. Barnes. "On school grounds you have defaced a private vehicle and who knows how long it will take to clean that limo, not to mention *how* inappropriate."

I nod as she talks. "School grounds." Nod. "Clean." Nod. "Inappropriate." Nod. *Yes, I get it. All too well, Mrs. Barnes. It's you who doesn't understand how serious this is, Mrs. Barnes. You don't understand anee-thing.*

It's freezing but I feel hot, almost feverish. It's like a heat wave is racing up my spine. The floor almost shakes and I can still hear the thrumming of the music through the closed doors.

The Importance of Being Ernestine

I stare at Mrs. Barnes's Master of Education degree

from the University of California at Davis and her Best Volleyball Coach Ever plaque. Her office isn't that big and I feel like I'm suffocating. My stomach ricochets and I REALLY need some air. My whole body feels chilled and hot at the same time and little pinpricks of energy swirl even down to my toes. "I—don't feel very well," I mumble.

"I can see you'll be fine. Too many Cokes. That's why you fainted at the dance. You of all people, my dear, have nothing to feel sick about."

That's it. I'm Mount Vesuvius. Pompei. "Yes, I do! I'm stuck in this heinous body forever!"

Mrs. Barnes screws up her face so that her eyes practically come together. "Taffeta Smith, you're many things." She makes little quote marks in the air. "But quote, unquote, 'heinous' is not one of them."

"Did you just call me Taffeta?"

"Yes." *Uh-huh.*

"Taffeta? Taffeta Smith?"

"That is your name."

"Do you have a mirror?" She opens her purse and hands me a compact. I see hazel eyes, an upturned nose, and hair that does not frizz. I see *me.*

"Omigod! I love you!" I throw my arms around

her. The woman is sort of rigid but she relents.

"What's this about, Taffeta?"

"I . . . just had to tell you I love your dress!" I'm filled with cheery goodness. "This school! This planet!" I need to get back to the dance. I want my friends to know that I'm back. I am running through the courtyard when I stop cold in front of a planter full of a straggly bush with Christmas lights. Wait a minute. Which friends do I tell? I know what to do and nearly skip into the gym. Not skip. FLY!

I'm Back!

I stop Olivia and Ninai as they're about to head over to the refreshment table. My former domain. "I'm so glad to see you," I say all out of breath, even though I'm back in my in-shape body. "You won't believe it. Something worked. Look, I'm me. Go ahead. Pinch me. It's me. It worked out. It's my skin. My legs. And hair and it's all silky and everything. Feel." *Wait a minute. Olivia is definitely not dancing with Winslow anymore. I'm so confused. I mean, why did I turn back? It's not like I actually, technically, danced with Winslow.*

"Um, Taffeta," says Olivia, inching away. "You do have very nice hair and all."

Ninai rolls her eyes at Olivia. "Very nice." They

both have face paint on. Olivia looks like a kangaroo and Ninai appears to be a walrus. No lip gloss, hairstyles, knee-high leather boots. None of it.

"Ninai, Olivia?" I moan. "Don't you remember me at all?"

"Why are you talking to us?" asks Olivia.

"Because you're my friends."

"Yeah, right, Taffeta, and there's a paper you'd like to copy," says Olivia. "A test coming up, or would you like to speak to him?" She points to Winslow who's shuffling over toward us.

"No, you guys don't understand. We're *good* friends now! You promised you'd go biking with me."

"Now?"

Oh, man. I forget I'm back in my original world, my true self, whatever that is. My hair is long and unfrizzy. In the blinking disco lights, I notice I'm wearing Juicy jeans and a lacy crop top. "Okay, I know I sound like a freak, but we've been friends for a few weeks now and I really like you guys. I mean it."

I can feel the distrust radiating off their bodies. Then my eye catches something, a calligraphy *E*. I am wearing the scarf that Olivia and Ninai gave me. It's the only thing that survived in the transformation. That's so weird.

"Look, I'm sorry for everything. All of those e-mails last year pretending Tyler liked you. I was mean and stupid and if I could take it ALL back I would. Tyler had nothing to do with it. I've been a jerk, and I want to make it up to you. I want to be your friend. But the truth is, Olivia, Tyler isn't who I thought he was exactly."

Ninai and Olivia's eyes pop open. Olivia takes a step backward, as if I couldn't possibly be for real. "There's so much that I want to tell you. Like the reason that Mrs. Barnes is doing the testing in January. Ninai, you have to organize a school protest or something. Olivia, it's because she wants to test when a lot of the ESL students will be visiting their families down in Mexico!" I think I'm screaming this info because even with the rocking-out music, heads are turning. I could swear I can even see Caylin peering at me. After all, I'm talking about Principal Barnes, her mother.

Ninai and Olivia stare at each other like they don't know what to make of this info. "If this is true," says Ninai. "It's *very* serious. You better not be trying to scam us into doing something stupid."

"No," I say. "I swear. After the dance is over,

I'll call you guys and tell you everything I heard. Seriously."

I watch Olivia scrunch up her face in confusion and Ninai shake her head. *Are they getting this? Me?* I'm not sure.

Winslow waltzes up to me, giving me a withering look, like he'd like to turn me into a ghost in that stupid game of his and take all of my gold and suck up all of my life force. Winslow gazes back at Olivia and Ninai and then at me. "Do you have another test or something? Do you need to cheat off one of us?" Winslow pushes up his glasses. And he's still, thankfully, himself. The T-shirt with a weird, funny saying, his chain jangling, duct tape still on his shoes. He's sporting his usual ponytail and love patch.

The same, but better-looking somehow, maybe just to me.

Go Away!

Olivia fiddles with the jingle bells on her skirt. She squints hard at me and Winslow sneers at me. I glance back and forth between Olivia and Winslow. They aren't even standing remotely close to each other. "So why aren't you guys dancing?" I ask.

Winslow squints at Olivia and Olivia squints at Winslow.

"With him?" she asks. "Sure, why not?" She shrugs.

I thought she'd be more enthusiastic than that. I'm confused.

Winslow scoots backward from me and throws his hands in the air. "Don't worry, I'm not even near you, Taffeta," says Winslow. "I won't ask you to dance, *ma chérie*. I know how you feel about me. You made it perfectly clear when you reneged on the deal you made with me in social studies. You must have been desperate when you said you'd go to Winterfest with me if I let you cheat off me on that test. I get it. I won't mess up *le reputation*. I am *le mold* and you are *le royalty*." Winslow backs farther away from me, both hands in the pockets of his black jeans. Turning around, I can see SpongeBob underwear sticking out.

"No. No!" I yell, but it's too late. He disappears into the crowd.

I glance at the wall of dance grams written on pink stars, snowmen, blue and yellow snowballs.

Petra, I love you, Caylin!

Hey Girls, Want to see my Snowflake?
The Guy
To Winslow, you 're the coolest. From Winslow

A sea of faces. I close my eyes because it's too much. I can only hear voices. I have no idea who is saying what to who or what it all means.

I continue to read the wall of messages.

Hey, chica, love you always and 4 ever. Thanks for being one of my best friends

To my choochi

One long message especially catches my eye.

Taffeta,
When you walk down the hall
You look like le mall
Your smile not so nice
It must be frozen in ice
You 're think you 're so hot
Well, you can just rot
So beautiful, so tall
Are you human at all?

P.S. Sure, Taffeta is considered high-end fabric but the word comes from Persian and means "twisted."

He Hates Me!

Winslow! He hates me! I can't believe I miss Ernestine. I want her back. I want her back with Winslow and Olivia and Ninai and . . .

Tyler shuffles up to me and Caylin pushes me into him. "Go for it!" Maggie the Mushroom, who's next to Caylin, starts giggling.

"Stop it!" I say to Caylin. "And don't even think about trying to set up Olivia with Tyler as a joke because it's not really that funny. Okay?"

"Whatever," says Caylin, who rolls her eyes at Maggie the Mushroom. "You're the one who wrote all of the e-mails."

"Olivia?" says Tyler, running his fingers through his green hair.

"Yes, Olivia, the medieval Russian one with the hair in her face."

Pink bleeds into Tyler's pale cheeks. "Oh, her. She's kind of interesting."

Her? Kind of interesting. I'm shocked he's said this out loud and I can see that Olivia and Ninai are too. They're standing in the bleachers only a few feet away from us. And there's a break between songs so it's actually quiet. Maybe I'm really going to have change my opinion of Tyler.

"How about it, Taf?" Tyler says, "Wanna dance?" A song starts up again.

"No, Tyler."

"'No, Tyler?'"

"I like someone else."

"That's cool."

"It's not cool. Not everything's cool, impervious." He looks shocked and I'm happy. There, I did it. I used a big word publicly, and I feel exhilarated.

And, suddenly, I'm noticing that Tyler is sidling over to the bleachers toward Oliva—like, he's standing so close his arm is brushing hers.

And Olivia is staring directly into my eyes and then glancing at Tyler like she's seeing a mirage.

Then Ninai strides over to me, cupping her head so she can be heard above the music. "I believe you. About Mrs. Barnes, I think. During break, let's meet at my house. We've got some letters to write."

"I think Caylin will want in on this too," I say.

Ninai lifts her eyebrows. "Caylin? But Mrs. Barnes is her mother. Are you serious?"

I bite my bottom lip. "Uh-huh."

Ninai glances over at Olivia and Tyler, who are now playfully hip-bumping each other. "Apparently, miracles are happening everywhere tonight." She lowers her voice. "Olivia has had a secret crush on Tyler for about a year. I know that's like a joke to you. She's been trying to get over Tyler and convince herself it's Winslow she really wants, but I don't think it's really working." *Whoa! Rock my world!* So my fake love e-mails from Tyler to Olivia must have made Olivia's day. Our joke on Olivia is seeming even less funny.

I suddenly need to change the subject. "You know I really actually like algebra. And I'm thinking about volunteering in the library with you Book Worms after school. I like unicorn books." I go for blurtation. "Especially Ann McCaffrey. But *The Last Unicorn* by Theodore Sturgeon is a masterpiece."

Ninai grins and I smile back at her.

"Me too. I love unicorns," parrots Maggie the Mushroom, and I have to say, some things never change.

Last Dance?

I march up to the DJ and whisper to put on a slow song. He listens to me. Everyone listens to Taffeta. It's a slow song. I peer through the crowd, desperately searching for Winslow. He doesn't seem to be anywhere on the dance floor. It's hard to miss Winslow because he's pretty much taller and wider than anyone at school, except for Mrs. Gibbons, one of the gym teachers. I stand up on my tiptoes, craning my neck. Finally, I see a large hulking figure on all fours in front of the sound system. Typical techie, of course. As the bass from the amps booms in my ears, I sidle right up to Winslow. "Want to dance?"

"Very funny," he growls.

"No, I'm serious. We have a dance to finish . . . start."

"Yeah, whatever. Limo girl."

"I don't care about the limo." I turn around and commence blurtation: "ANYONE WHO WANTS A FREE RIDE IN A LIMO, GO TO THE PARKING LOT." (I seriously see Ms. Stuckley and Mrs. Grund rush for the limo.)

Winslow hoods his face with his hand like he's looking at me from across the sea. I know he's not getting anee-thing.

"I'm a girl who's seen another world," I desperately explain. "Another possibility. And it's made me realize things about me that I don't like and realize that I've made some mistakes . . . and I apologize, Winslow. Really. I . . . I was an idiot. I want to be your friend. I've learned all kinds of things about you. Like you're a black belt in tae kwon do and use your notebook to help when you assist the dojo. In your house, on your kitchen island you keep a butcher block of knives that isn't exactly stable, and your first pet was Fluffy, and the first street you lived on was on Harrington Place. And you have a tendency to go after girls who look good from far away, but if you look on the inside I'm not so sure. But then again your mom is 'corporate hot.'"

Winslow closes his eyes and opens them again. "Okay. That's weird. I'm not going to ask because . . ." He gazes over to where Tyler and Olivia are actually talking, her hennaed head close to his albino green one. Her blouse billows like a cotton cloud. I can see her crooked-toothed smile. Once again Winslow's eyes dart over to Tyler and Olivia. "Did you . . . are you responsible for . . . ?"

I nod.

He peers at me, probing my face.

I place my arms around his neck. "What's your answer?" I ask him.

"What's the question?" he asks.

"Do you want to dance?"

"Okay, *larve d'ejection*," Winslow says.

"'Larve d'ejection'?"

"*Oui*, your name in French. Tafetta is a kind of silk made from larva." He spreads out his arms. "I don't get you, but I'm not going to try." His hands go around my waist. It's a slow song, and everybody, and I mean *everybody,* watches us dance. They stop, actually. I don't think anyone else is really dancing in the place. Meshell-at-the-beach and other invisibles sway to the music.

Mushroom and Caylin gape as the two of us dance very closely. Suddenly, Caylin breaks away and sidles up to me.

As I'm dancing with Winslow, she whispers in my ear. "I heard what you said about my mother." For a moment, every muscle clenches together. My body feels like one tight fist.

Winslow glances at me funny because it's like the three of us are slow-dancing.

"And I can't believe she'd do something like that," says Caylin. "There just has to be a misunderstanding. I think someone should just talk to her, right? Before, like, making a big deal, right? Okay?" Her eyes are watery. "I never could stand cheating. Ever. Every time you and Petra do it, I feel like throwing up, okay.

Okay? Do you believe me? 'Cause that's how I feel."

I look at her Tahoe blue eyes and perky, but now blotchy, face. "Actually, I didn't know that's how you felt. But thanks for telling me. We'll talk about it later. Okay?" Maybe that would explain all of her stomachaches all of the time.

As she moves away, I gaze up at Winslow. "I'm so sorry. There's totally something I gotta do for a sec." Winslow nods as I pull away for a moment to give Caylin a quick hug. After I take a breath, and head back to Winslow, I notice my mother trying to act inconspicuous. With two cameras slung around her neck, she stands in the corner next to a giant stack of folding chairs. I'm so happy that she's here. I want to share this moment of aliveness with her. It's like I can feel all of my cells in my skin dancing.

"That's *my* MOM!" I shout. "Phyllis!" I blow her a kiss. "She's a great photographer! C'mon, Mom. Get some close-ups of my friends!" I pull over to where Ninai and Sneed, Olivia and Tyler, and a few others are all dancing. They actually smile at me. Then I hop on over to Winslow and we dance to a hip-hop song that I really like called "'*The Avenue*.'"

My mom looks so happy. I mean it. She's grinning and snapping photos and, yes, has brought with her these giant lights and I don't care. Let her snap away. She's actually pretty good at it. I mean, she's only been doing this for a half a year and I think she might be on to something. "That's my mom, everybody!" I shout.

Caylin turns around and gives her gummy smile. A few of the Mushroom's friends wave at my mom, who's not wearing pajama bottoms and her hair has been brushed. But that doesn't matter. If she wants to wear her pj's, that's her deal. She's an artist. Artists are supposed to be quirky.

And I actually almost wore pajamas to school once, didn't I? Maybe I will actually do it again. Then, of course, it will become a TREND.

A Fresh Start

I spot Dribble in the corner and I actually mouth *thank you* to him. And then I notice he's standing there in that corner, eating a pimpled pickle, talking to my mom all animated-like, as if they already know each other WELL. But why is he talking to my mom? My heart speed-races and I apologize to Winslow again, beg him to stay put, and zoom over to where they are standing next to the bleachers by the exit sign to check out what I'm seeing, because it is dark in here with lots of colored disco lights that could make me hallucinate. As I approach, they are *still* talking. He's whispering in her ear and then she turns, cupping her hand, whispering back like they're in middle school or something. I plant myself right in front, and that's when they turn to me. "Do you two know each other?" I demand.

Mom puts her hands on Mr. Dribble's shoulder. "Cosmically and spiritually."

It's like one of the disco lights has lasered my gut because this is disgusting. Could Mr. Dribble actually be my mom's secret boyfriend or something? Mom fiddles with a camera knob. "Mr. Drabner is my medium; I thought you knew that."

"Medium. He's your . . . medium. Mr. Dribble, *your* . . ." The little wheels—I guess rusty wheels—start creaking and I get it. I mean GET IT because Mr. Dribble's name comes to me. John T. Drabner. The *T* probably stands for Tosh! And then his "consulting business," and that's why he loved Winslow's MEDIUM joke T-shirt. I peer at him, with his bushy mustache and plastered-down comb-over, through completely new eyes. "You're Mom's Tosh. *You*." I nod over at Mom who's giggling and shaking her head. "She listens to you. I'm just getting this now."

"I know," says Dribble/Tosh, hobbling closer to

me. "Easy-peasy pie." He stuffs the last bite of pickle into his mouth.

"Why did I turn back earlier? At that point, I hadn't actually danced with Winslow."

"I asked you if you behaved in ways toward folks you'd like to rectify. Anyhoo, Winslow wasn't the only one."

I think about all of those mean e-mails I wrote from Tyler to Olivia and the way that I used to treat her. And then I think about what had happened on the dance floor. Me sacrificing for Olivia. Maybe I had rectified. Ah, I'm getting it a little, but not everything. As I finger my scarf, the only thing left from the Ernestine world, Tosh/Dribble says, "Like your little souvenir?"

Honesty

Caylin jumps up and down, waving. I know I have my friend back. She's not crying anymore. She's as good as me at covering up her emotions. Maggie the Mushroom is gushing at Caylin. I have to admit I love it when Maggie gushes, except for the saliva. She says it has something to do with her braces, but I think she has an overactive salivary gland or something. With all of the foam coming out of the corner of her mouth, I worry that someday she's going to get penned up for rabies.

"It is amazing what passes for popular at this school sometimes," I say to Winslow as we continue to dance again.

Caylin stands there staring at us dancing. Since kindergarten I've been expecting lots of attention when I turned fourteen at the first dance with a boy that I liked. Of course, I didn't expect it to be a boy like Winslow.

"Girls," says Caylin. "Am I seeing what I'm seeing?" Mushroom covers her mouth, studying Tyler and Olivia, me and Winslow. "Unbelievable."

But then when Caylin sees that I'm serious, that it is not a joke, she smiles and changes her tune. The girl is definitely loyal. "You know, Winslow is sorta interesting-looking. You can really see the potential."

Mushroom smiles so that her dimples pock her cheeks. "I bet with his size, if he worked out he could play football and look *really* awesome."

Why?

"Why are you doing this?" asks Winslow.

"Why did you like me?" I ask Winslow. "Answer me."

"Because. Look at you." He pulls away from me and smiles at what he sees.

"Okay. Look at me. So?"

"You're, you know. You want me to say it?" He gulps and his Adam's apple bobbles for a moment.

"There must be OTHER reasons," I say.

"Other reasons? You look mysterious. Like maybe you understood me."

"Go on."

"I saw how everyone comes up to you, which is intriguing."

"Same with you," I admit. "They want something from you."

"Yeah, so."

"That's what it's like for me." His breath smells like Cool Ranch tortilla chips. I suddenly remember how much I like ranch dressing. He stops dancing and stares at me with his Saturn eyes. You know what? I think I have a shot at becoming Chewbacca's girlfriend.

Suddenly, I have a crazy urge to kiss him, so I go for further blurtation. "But sometimes, you need a chance to be someone else for a while to know what you really want. Who you really are. That's why you do that online video game, right? To be someone else."

He pauses. "Yeah . . . that's true."

And then I think I've blown it because he's pulling away from me, a bit stiffly, like maybe he's unsure of something, so I just do it, with EVERYONE watching. I kiss Winslow Fromes, for the second time in my life, but this time he's kissing me back and, for a moment, I'm not in the gym, in a middle school with a bad speaker system. It's an alone moment, and I'm all right with that. More than all right, so I whisper in his ear, "Let's just be us for a while. Okay?"

Winslow's hands pull tighter around my waist. "Whatever that is."

Then this overweight girl comes whirling up to me. She's got greasy hair and glasses that are smudged and her pants are so high-water they could almost be shorts. I feel sorry for her as she desperately reads the messages on the wall, probably hoping someone out there wrote one for her. Suddenly, she grabs my arm. "I don't see my name anywhere," she moans, practically in tears.

"Sorry, I don't know who you are," I say, trying to help. "Tell me your name."

"I should be EVERYWHERE ON THIS WALL!" She points to where all the messages are posted. "But, Taffeta, I just read them all and I'm not there."

I can tell by the indignation, it's Petra.

Just like me, she's finally and undeniably gotten her fresh start.